The Jinx

The Jinx

Théophile Gautier

Translated by Andrew Brown

ET REMOTISSIMA PROPE

100 PAGES

100 PAGES
Published by Hesperus Press Limited
4 Rickett Street, London SW6 1RU
www.hesperuspress.com

First published by Hesperus Press Limited, 2002

Introduction and English language translation © Andrew Brown, 2002
Foreword © Gilbert Adair, 2002

Designed and typeset by Fraser Muggeridge
Printed in the United Arab Emirates by Oriental Press

ISBN: 1-84391-020-9

CONTENTS

FOREWORD

An eerie little masterpiece about a rationalist gradually persuaded of the existence of the irrational, *The Jinx* – or, to give the original French (or rather Italian) title, *Jettatura* – is perhaps the finest of a handful of supernatural tales written in the mid-nineteenth century by the poet and novelist Théophile Gautier... And the first question a potential modern reader, intrigued yet sceptical, will most likely pose is: Théophile who?

Poor Gautier. His fiction has ceased to be much read and his best-known volume of verse bears a title, *Emaux et camées* [*Enamels and Cameos*], which for all its euphonious glamour is redolent of an irretrievably dated conception of literary aestheticism. Even his name has now become a signifier of oblivion. To a contemporary French ear 'Théophile' has just as fustily outmoded a ring as 'Theophilus' to a British one; and the surname 'Gautier' is remembered above all as that of Marguerite, the Lady of the Camelias, in Alexandre Dumas *fils*' hoary old warhorse.

Yet Gautier was one of the great *animateurs* of the nineteenth-century French cultural scene, akin to Jean Cocteau or even Andy Warhol in the twentieth. He was actually present at the première of Victor Hugo's *Hernani*, the most scandalous in Parisian theatrical history – not only present but conspicuous in his famous blood-red waistcoat. A passionate balletomane, he was responsible for the libretto or 'argument' (as it's properly called, doubtless with very good reason) of Adolphe Adam's *Giselle*, the most enduring of all pre-Tchaikovskian ballets. He was the privileged dedicatee of Baudelaire's *Les Fleurs du mal*. And he was a supreme master of what the French refer to as the *conte fantastique*.

As a stylist, Gautier was something of a dandy, a forerunner of Wilde, with whom he shared a predilection (that title, *Emaux et camées*) for individual words as rare as precious gems. By comparison with Gautier, however, Wilde was a vulgarian, campily salivating over eglantines and asphodels. The Frenchman was more of a dandy in the Beau Brummel mode. Complimented on his sartorial elegance at Ascot, Brummel allegedly replied, 'If you noticed me, I couldn't have been elegant', a comment which might equally be made of Gautier's prose, with its innate distaste for gaudy adjectival cuff-links and cravat pins.

The Jinx, like most of his short stories, belongs to a sub-genre of the *conte fantastique* that was dubbed by the witty author himself 'fantasy in a frock-coat'. And it's this distinction which elevates his work above that of his rivals who, in derivative thrall to 'Hoffmania', the craze for the tales of E.T.A. Hoffmann that swept literary Europe in the 1850s, had a tendency to borrow too liberally from a lexicon of supernatural props and properties made fashionable by the German fantasist and his numerous imitators – elves, wilis, imps, *succubi*, vampires, doppelgänger, etc. What Gautier brought to a genre which was even in its heyday regarded by some sniffy critics as marginal and faintly disreputable (Hoffmann notwithstanding) was a high stylistic sheen. The effect on us now, as on his contemporaries then, is to render the supernatural element, when it eventually materialises, all the more unexpected.

Consider *The Jinx*. Even if its theme is *jettatura*, the 'evil eye', it repudiates absolutely the pulpy bric-à-brac of subliterary sensationalism, which is precisely why its narrative is so unsettling. In fact, if there's a single determinant factor in the malaise which the novella induces in the reader, it is, precisely, the sober brio of Gautier's style. Thus: when the protagonist, Paul d'Aspremont, a Frenchman as refined as the language that brings him alive on the page, arrives in noisy, smelly, pagan Naples to join his virginal English fiancée, the fastidious imperturbability of Gautier's storytelling voice, so like d'Aspremont's own, immediately invites us to identify with him. When, subsequently, the young dandy's aplomb, aloofness and cold, penetrating gaze – all words applicable to the very idiom in which these traits are described – cause him to be accused of possessing the evil eye, we are again tempted to follow his example and dismiss such accusations as nothing more than the superstitious prejudices of an excitable race. And even when, no longer so sure of himself, he feverishly sets about reinterpreting the whole of his past life in the light of this apparent curse, like someone who 'opens a medical book, either by chance or to pass the time, and on reading the pathological description of an illness, recognises that he is afflicted by it.' It is the unruffled poise of Gautier's prose that encourages us to remain firmly and, as it turns out, complacently in the camp of rationality. Which is when the author abruptly pulls the carpet out from underneath our – and d'Aspremont's – feet.

Here, then, we have a flawless specimen of 'fantasy in a frock-coat'. For it was Gautier's genius to have understood that, although we may be less and less willing (and we are even less willing nowadays than in his own day) to suspend our collective disbelief when confronted by the formulaic and moth-eaten motifs of older, more traditional versions of the supernatural, we can still be disturbed by the insidious encroachment of that supernatural on the textures and trappings of the natural world. We still find genuinely unnerving the contamination of the explicable by the inexplicable and, in the specific case of *The Jinx*, the contamination of the rational (Gautier's style) by the irrational (his subject-matter).

To depict his hero's blade in the climactic duel, one of the most hauntingly surreal in nineteenth-century fiction (and it was, as we know, a golden age of literary duels), Gautier has recourse to an incongruous conjunction of adverb and adjective: 'curiously terrifying'. Well, given that for most of us a monster in a frock-coat is inherently scarier than one with horns, scales and claws, *The Jinx* in its entirety proves to be a curiously terrifying work.

– Gilbert Adair, 2002

INTRODUCTION

In the twentieth century, a curious superstition started to spread. It decreed that the source of so many of the world's ills could be located, quite simply, in the gaze. The mere activity of looking at something was considered destructive. The gaze, it was said, converted the rich and living variety of the world into an assembly of inert, mortified things, displayed for the predatory delectation of the eyes of insatiable spectators. Modern technologies – photography, cinema, television, computer screens – filled the world with a riot of images that the gaze, when not overmastered by such profligacy of vision feasted on with lustful voyeurism. The gaze was an agent of power: it seemed as if the whole of human history was merely the record of all the ways in which the gaze had separated itself out from other senses, and assumed a dominant and fateful role as universal spymaster. To look back, to return the gaze, was simply to reinforce its fascinating power. 'Big Brother is Watching You' (even when – especially when – you are watching *Big Brother*).

Social geography, it appeared, had always been in thrall to the gaze, whose main function was to ensure clean lines of sight for authority to pry on the activities of a populace kept under constant surveillance. The boulevards of Baron Haussmann in mid-nineteenth century Paris, and the closed-circuit TV that by the late twentieth century was starting to become such a ubiquitous presence, were merely two of the most recent additions to power's panoramic desire to see and master everything. When turned in this way on living human beings, or 'subjects', the gaze, even without touching them in any other way, could kill them, or at least, in some symbolic way, convert them into 'objects'.

It was indeed modern Paris that was home to the most fervent devotees of the superstition (and the most eloquent proponents of its central tenets). But some of their articles of faith were survivals, not always acknowledged, of much older beliefs. The gaze was an essentially masculine activity, predicated on the powers and aggressive desires of men and exercised, usually, against women, so that to look was to be a man, and to be looked at was to be either a woman or, at the very least, feminised, or symbolically castrated: this slide from just looking to actual rape seemed to echo words spoken two millennia previously: 'whosoever looketh on a woman to lust after her hath committed adultery with her already in his heart' (Matthew, 5:28). The seminar rooms and lecture halls of the Latin Quarter were filled with anxious students debating how the fearful threat of the gaze (powerful, panoptic, and penetrating; masculine, menacing, and murderous) could be tamed. Few went so far as to decide that the only remedy was the drastic one recommended in the succeeding verse from St Matthew: 'if thy right eye offend thee, pluck it out' (or let someone else do it for you).

The most that could be hoped, in the absence of any charm or talisman to ward off the rampaging gaze, was the ritual murmuring of certain phrases and the deployment of a battery of terms that could be fingered like a lucky charm when the gaze's presence was sensed to be near: it was, they muttered, the agent of reification, or commodification, or fetishisation, creating a mere society of the spectacle (the jargon used by those who lived in dread of the gaze, the so-called 'scopophobes', varied depending on the sect to which they belonged). In any event, the superstition, recognisable above all by its language, soon spread throughout the civilised world: the 'Age of Anxiety' was above all the age of a demonic gaze which had become so all-pervasive and all-powerful so as no longer to be the gaze of any one person or even any one group, but almost a transcendental precondition for there to be anything at all. In this way, the modern superstition repeated earlier, prescientific notions (the Aristotelian and scholastic belief that the eye did not so much receive as emit rays of life; the view of Bishop Berkeley that 'to be is to be perceived'), embellishing them with the still largely misunderstood 'indeterminacy principle' which was interpreted to mean that you could change things – always for the worse, in the view of the scopophobes – just by looking at them.

What I have called a 'superstition' is of course, in many ways, a perfectly justifiable belief (or, to put it another way, I too am to some extent a scopophobe). That the gaze all too often establishes a gradient of power (seeing often *is* a way of dominating and controlling), gender (seeing often *is* more masculine than feminine), violence (seeing often *is* the first step to rape and murder), and that at the very least it tends to objectify what it rests on, depriving it of life, autonomy and subject-hood, is indisputable.

Gautier's story *The Jinx* reminds us that the obsession with averting the gaze or, as it has more often been called, the evil eye, is deeply rooted in many human societies. It also suggests that we may be no more justified in calling the '*jettatura*' or 'jinx' a mere superstition than we would be in applying the same label, as I ironically and reductively did above, to the modern fear of the gaze. In this story, the protagonist Paul d'Aspremont is afflicted by the evil eye – something he realises only belatedly, and to his horror; and something whose malevolent effects on his beloved Miss Alicia Ward he attempts to ward off, first by seeking death in a duel where he refuses to take the slightest advantage from his poisonous gift over his opponent Count Altavilla, insisting on their both being blindfolded so that his deadly gaze will not cause his enemy to falter, and finally, quite literally, obeying the stern command in the Gospel, and blinding himself.

Alicia is a sturdy Protestant, sceptical of southern superstition, who refuses to believe both the accusations of Altavilla, and then the implicit self-accusations of d'Aspremont – that the latter is jinxing her, that by simply turning his adoring eyes on her beauty he is vampirically draining away her life-force. A fine example of the deadly masculine gaze at its most apparently innocent and really deadly, perhaps. At all events, Alicia becomes caught in the cross-fire between opposites: her modern, rationalised Christianity versus the archaic paganism of the '*jettatura*' or '*fascino*' (sometimes called '*malocchio*' or evil eye); her longing to be gazed at by Paul's loving eyes versus her awareness that his gaze may kill her; her faith, her true religion (which includes a degree of fatalistic acceptance of risk), versus the superstition which sees the world as in the grip of powerful, irrational forces that need to be – and can to a large extent be – placated and controlled by obsessional ritualistic gestures.

But there are other tensions determining her fate: those of the different national aesthetic tastes that, from at least the early nineteenth century onwards, were seen as springing from different climates. Originally a thriving English miss, she starts, under the gaze of the Frenchman d'Aspremont, to sicken and become akin to an Ossianic wraith; transplanted to an Italy whose luxuriant vegetation and sunshine she revels in, she blossoms into – as she jokes – a buxom Italian peasant-girl, anxious that her rosy cheeks now lack the distinguished pallor that Paul had initially found attractive, and that he unconsciously re-establishes in her now that he has come to Italy to see her again. But these polarities become entangled in chiasmus: if the north is all mists, consumption, and romantic idealisation, it is also reason, scepticism, and the beefsteak and rum of her devoted uncle; and if the south is sunshine, vulgar vitality, and classical realism, it is also superstition, credulity, and spooky premonition. Count Altavilla loquaciously defends the notion of '*jettatura*', convincing the at first no-nonsense commodore, and intriguing Alicia with the possibility that there are more things in heaven and earth than are dreamt of in her philosophy: he points out, sensibly enough, that a belief of such antiquity may well have its own rationality.

'Super-stition': what has survived from the past, been handed on, still stands. The need to draw a distinction between true faith and mere superstition, or between rational science and superstition, given the fact that neither faith nor reason are immune from the vagaries of cultural geography or the processes of history, with their attendant threat of relativism, is something the story constantly gestures towards. And yet Gautier refuses to endorse the belief in '*jettatura*' as such: every event for which it seems to be an explanation could also be explained by mere coincidence. The problem is that mere coincidence is not easy to depict in literature, which errs towards superstition (the craving for meaning at all costs) rather than towards a rationalism whose meanings often seem indistinguishable from meaninglessness, as in the modern scientific, positivist world-view.

Gautier's own aesthetic is balanced between the two. His poetry, notably the collection *Emaux et camées* (*Enamels and Cameos*, a title suggestive of rococo decorativeness), first published in 1852, often seems visual to the point of superficiality, and his love of craft made him a figurehead of the '*l'art pour l'art*' movement with its apologia for a beauty that often seemed inhuman, statuesque and objectified – the product of mere gazing, yet again. His love of the sculptural, of medals and coins, and his antiquarian interests, are strongly in evidence in *The*

Jinx, especially in the extraordinary climactic scene of the duel in Pompeii. So is his talent for portraying the visual world, as in the finely picturesque depiction of the Bay of Naples.

Gautier's skill at caricature, as in the colourful portrayal of English lords and Neapolitan servants, suggests indeed that a certain kind of visual realism can turn into the evil eye of stereotype. But his fantastic tales, of which *The Jinx* is one, show how easily a rather decorative realism can slide into uncanny premonition. The slow accumulation of at first rather minor mishaps that herald d'Aspremont's arrival in Naples is superbly handled, gradually modulating into the suspicion that they are not just realist details (the coincidental things that might just happen), but have their cause in d'Aspremont himself: once the idea of the *'jettatura'* has been mooted, we as readers are invited to share the *post hoc* interpretation of the Neapolitan servants and, superstitiously or not, entertain the belief that an unexpectedly high wave or a sudden downpour are the results of Paul's evil eye.

Gautier does not conclude for or against the credibility of the jinx. Alicia Ward, faced with its malevolent power, retreats from classical robustness to northern Gothic etherealism, and, although bravely prepared to sustain and even invite Paul's deadly gaze, is gradually transformed into a type of beauty too spiritual to survive. Indeed, she changes in appearance, like a casebook example from the aesthetics of Hegel, from this-worldly classicism to other-worldly romanticism, or from the clear outlines of Kant's 'beautiful' to the mistier and more abstract premonitions of his 'sublime', finally moving beyond the realm of appearance altogether.

Paul's gaze had been attracted by her visible beauty, but forces her into complete invisibility. He has already decided that he will no longer look on the world and its phenomenal beauties; when his eyes had drifted vacantly across the spectacle of life, all was well: it was when he looked more closely, through his pince-nez perhaps, or with amorous intensity, that he started to cause damage. Scopophobia may have its superstitious side, but there is a truth lurking in it. Gautier suggests, through Paul's tragic fate, that visual realism – the close and indeed loving perception of the world's phantasmagoria – can easily become harmful, petrifying and ossifying like the lava that captured and killed

Pompeii; the attempt to mute the force of that scrutiny may come too late, and literary verisimilitude, attempting just to show the way things happen to be, innocent of all imposed interpretation, cannot long avoid the pull of the superstition of meaning – the superstition (if that is the right word for it) which makes us human.

– Andrew Brown, 2002

Note on Publication Dates

Jettatura (*The Jinx*) was first published in 1857, and subsequently in book form (*Romans et contes*) in 1863. I have used the edition of the *Récits fantastiques* (Garnier-Flammarion: Paris, 1981, edited by Marc Eigeldinger).

The Jinx

CHAPTER ONE

The *Leopold*, a superb Tuscan steamboat which sailed between Marseilles and Naples, had just rounded the tip of Procida. The passengers were all out on deck, cured of their seasickness by the sight of land: a more effective cure than Malta sweets and other prescriptions used in such cases.

On the deck in the enclosure reserved for first-class passengers stood several Englishmen endeavouring to keep as far away from each other as possible and to draw around themselves an impassable circular boundary; their splenetic faces were carefully shaved, their neckties were perfectly free of creases, their stiff white shirt-collars resembled the corners of sheets of Bristol paper; fresh clean suede gloves were on their hands, and Lord Elliot's varnish gleamed on their brand new shoes. You would have said that they had emerged from one of the compartments of their travel bags; in their correct outfits were none of the minor traces of untidiness that are the ordinary consequence of travelling. Among them were lords, MPs, City merchants, Regent's Street tailors, and Sheffield cutlers, all respectable, all grave, all immobile, all bored. There was no lack of women either, for Englishwomen are not sedentary like the women of other countries, and take advantage of the slightest pretext to leave their island. Next to the young ladies and the married women – autumnal beauties with blotchy, streaked skins – there glowed, beneath their veils of blue gauze, young misses with strawberries-and-cream complexions, shining coils of blond hair, and long, white teeth, recalling the types popular in memento books, and proving that English engravings are innocent of the charge of dishonesty that is so often levelled against them. These charming persons were modulating, independently of each other, in the most delightful British accent, the sacramental phrase: '*Vedi Napoli e poi mori*', consulting their travel guides or jotting down their impressions in their notebooks, without paying the least attention to the Don Juanesque winks of a few self-satisfied Parisians who were prowling round them, while their irritated mamas murmured in low voices about French impropriety.

On the periphery of the aristocratic quarter were strolling, as they smoked their cigars, three or four young men whom it was easy to recognise, from their straw or grey-felt hats, their short bag jackets studded with broad horn buttons, and their huge drill trousers, as artists – an indication confirmed moreover by their Van Dyck moustaches, their hair curled like that of a Rubens model or their crew cuts like those of a Paolo Veronese; they were trying, but with quite another aim in view than the dandies, to capture a few profiles of those beauties whom their lack of fortune prevented them from getting any closer to, and this preoccupation distracted them somewhat from the magnificent panorama spread out before their eyes.

At the ship's prow, leaning against the rail or sitting on bundles of coiled rope, were groups of the poor third-class travellers, finishing off the provisions that seasickness had caused them to leave untouched, and not deigning to glance at the most admirable spectacle in the world; a feeling for nature is the privilege of cultivated minds not entirely absorbed in the material necessities of life.

The weather was fine; the blue waves unfurled in broad pleats, with hardly enough strength to erase the wake left by the boat; the smoke from the stack, forming the sole cloud in this splendid sky, slowly wafted away in light fleecy tufts, and the paddles of the wheels, thrashing round in a diamond haze on which the sun hung little rainbows, churned the water with joyful vigour, as if they had been aware of the proximity of the harbour.

That long line of hills which, from Posillipo to Vesuvius, delineates the marvellous gulf at the head of which Naples reposes like a sea nymph drying herself on the shore after her swim, was starting to show more clearly its violet undulations, and stood out more firmly from the dazzling blue of the sky; already a few white spots, piercing the dark landscape of the fields, betrayed the presence of villas scattered through the countryside. Sails of fishing boats returning to port were gliding over the smooth blue water like swans' feathers drifting in the breeze, a sign of human activity on the majestic solitude of the sea.

After a few rotations of the paddle wheel, the outlines of the Castel Sant'Elmo and the San Martino monastery came distinctly into view at the summit of the mountain against which Naples leans, above the domes of churches, the terraces of hotels, the roofs of houses, the façades of palaces, and the greenery of gardens, all still only vaguely sketched in the luminous haze. Soon the Castel dell'Ovo, squatting on its reef washed with foam, seemed to advance towards the steamboat, and the pier with its lighthouse stretched out like an arm holding a torch.

At the extremity of the bay, Vesuvius, now closer, exchanged the bluish tints that distance had swathed it in for more energetic and solid tones; its flanks showed the furrows of ravines and solidified lava flows, and from its truncated cone, as if from the holes in an incense-burner, there emerged, clearly visible, small jets of white smoke that a light breeze dispersed.

The boat had come into sight of Chiatamone, Pizzo Falcone, the quay of Santa Lucia lined by hotels, the Palazzo Reale with its rows of balconies, the Palazzo Nuovo flanked by its *moucharaby* towers, the Arsenal, and ships of every nation, their masts and spars jostling like the trees of a wood stripped of its leaves, when from his cabin emerged a passenger who had not showed himself once during the whole crossing, either because seasickness had confined him to his berth, or because he was too antisocial to wish to mingle with the rest of the travellers, or else because this spectacle, new to most of them, had been familiar to him for a long time and offered him no further interest.

He was a young man of between twenty-six and twenty-eight, or at least that was the age you were tempted to ascribe to him at first glance, for when you looked at him more attentively you found him either younger or older, to such an extent was his enigmatic expression a mixture of freshness and fatigue. His dark blond hair was that shade of colour the English call auburn, and in the sunlight it blazed with a coppery, metallic sheen, while in the shade it appeared almost black; his profile was composed of cleanly drawn lines: a forehead with such pro-tuberances as would have attracted the admiration of a phrenologist, a nobly curving aquiline nose, finely moulded lips, and a powerfully rounded chin reminiscent of ancient medals; and yet all these features, handsome in themselves, did not add up to an attractive whole. They lacked that mysterious harmony which smoothes out the contours and blends them together. Legend speaks of an Italian painter who, wishing to depict the rebel archangel, composed for him a mask of disparate beauties, and thus achieved an effect of terror much greater than if he had resorted to horns, circumflex eyebrows, and a grinning mouth. The stranger's face produced an effect of this kind. His eyes in particular were extraordinary; the black lashes that bordered them contrasted with the light grey colour of his irises and the burnt brown tones of his hair. The thinness of the bones in his nose made these eyes seem set more closely together than the proportions established by the principles of drawing allow, and, as for their expression, it was quite indefinable. When they were gazing into space, a vague melancholy, a fondly lethargic expression could be read in them, and they had a moist gleam; if they focused on any person or object, the brows came together, contracted, and carved a perpendicular crease in the skin of his forehead: his irises, turning from grey to green, became speckled with black spots and streaked with yellow fibrils; his gaze flashed from them, piercing and almost wounding; then all resumed its initial placidity, and this character with his Mephistophelean appearance turned back into a young man of the world – a member of the Jockey Club, if you like – going to spend the season at Naples, and happy to set foot on lava paving-stones less likely to rise and fall than the deck of the *Leopold*.

His clothes were elegant without drawing attention to themselves by any showiness of detail: a dark blue frock-coat, a black polka-dot cravat whose knot was tied in a manner neither affected nor negligent, a waistcoat of the same design as the cravat, light grey trousers, beneath which was a fine pair of boots; the chain holding his watch was all of gold, and his pince-nez dangled from a cord of flat silk; his hand, elegantly gloved, was tapping a small slender cane in twisted vine stock, tipped with ornamental silver.

He strolled a few paces along the deck, allowing his gaze to wander vaguely towards the approaching shore along which carriages were rolling, the populace was swarming and, stationed here and there, groups of idlers for whom the arrival of a stagecoach or a steamboat is always an interesting and novel spectacle even though they have gazed at it a thousand times before.

Already a squadron of dinghies and rowing boats was launching out from the quay, preparing to assault the *Leopold*, laden with crews of hotel waiters, domestic staff, *facchini* [1] and other various kinds of riff-raff in the habit of considering foreigners as their prey; each boat was rowing its hardest to get there first, and the mariners were exchanging, as was their custom, insults and vociferous shouts capable of alarming anyone unacquainted with the manners of the Neapolitan lower class.

The young man with auburn hair had set his double pince-nez on his nose in order to see more clearly the scene unfolding before him; but his attention, distracted from the sublime spectacle of the bay by the concert of cries and complaints rising from the flotilla, focused on the dinghies; doubtless he found the noise disturbing, for his brows contracted, the crease in his forehead deepened, and the grey of his eyes took on a yellow hue.

An unexpected wave, sweeping along from the open sea, fringed with foam, passed under the steamboat – which it lifted and then dropped heavily – and broke against the quay in millions of points of glittering light, drenching the strollers who were taken completely by surprise at this sudden shower, and with the violence of its backwash making the boats clash so violently into one another that three or four *facchini* fell into the water. The accident was not serious, as those rascals can all swim like fish or sea-gods, and a few seconds later they reappeared, their hair plastered across their foreheads, spitting out the salty water through their mouths and blowing it through their nostrils, and, no doubt, just as astonished by their sudden dip as Telemachus, son of Ulysses, must have been when Minerva, in the shape of the wise Mentor, threw him from a rock into the sea so as to wrest him from the love of Eucharis.[2]

Behind the strange traveller, at a respectful distance, next to a great heap of travelling trunks, stood a little groom, a kind of old man at fifteen years of age, a gnome in livery, resembling those dwarf trees that the patient Chinese cultivate in vases to prevent them growing; his flat face, in which the nose hardly stuck out at all, seemed to have been squashed in infancy, and his prominent eyes had that mildness which certain naturalists find in those of a toad. His shoulders were not hunched or rounded, and his chest did not protrude; and yet he made you think of a hunchback, though you would have searched in vain for his hump. In short, he was a very respectable groom, who would have been able without further training to present himself at the Ascot or Chantilly races; any gentleman rider would have accepted him because of his ill-favoured appearance. He was unattractive, but irreproachable in his kind, just like his master.

The passengers disembarked; the porters, after more than Homeric exchanges of insults, divided the foreigners and their baggage up between them, and set off for the different hotels with which Naples is abundantly provided.

The traveller with the pince-nez and his groom made their way to the hotel Roma, followed by a large phalanx of robust *facchini* who pretended to pant and sweat under the weight of a hatbox or a light carton, hoping naively for a more generous tip, while five or six of their comrades, flexing muscles as powerful as those of the statue of Hercules you can admire at the Studii[3], pushed along a handcart in which bounced around two trunks of ordinary size and moderate weight.

When they had reached the door of the hotel and the *padron di casa* had designated to the new arrival the apartment he was to occupy, the porters, although they had received about three times the price of their errand, broke out into frenetic gesticulations and speeches in which the formulas of supplication were mixed with threats in the most comical proportions; they all spoke at once, with alarming volubility, demanding a larger tip, and swearing by their great gods that they had not been sufficiently recompensed for their labours.

Paddy, left alone to confront them – for his master, without bothering about this din, had already climbed the stairs – resembled a monkey surrounded by a pack of baying mastiffs: trying to calm this tumultuous hullabaloo, he harangued them for a short while in his mother tongue, that is, English. The harangue had little effect. So, clenching his fists and raising his arms up to chest height, with great precision he struck the pose of a boxer, to the loud hilarity of the *facchini*, and with a straight jab worthy of Adams or Tom Cribbs[4], and aiming right at the pit of the stomach, he sent the giant of the band tumbling backwards, arms and legs in the air, onto the lava paving-stones of the street.

This exploit put the troop to flight; the colossus heavily picked himself up, quite shaken by his fall; and without trying to take his revenge on Paddy, he went off, rubbing the bluish bruise that was starting to spread its rainbow hues across his skin with his hand and grimacing, convinced that a demon must be lurking under the jacket of that ugly monkey who looked as if the only animal he would be good at riding was not a horse but a dog, and whom, he had imagined, a mere breath should have been enough to flatten.

The stranger, having summoned the *padron di casa*, asked him whether a letter addressed to Monsieur Paul d'Aspremont had been delivered to the hotel Roma; the hotelier replied that a letter bearing that inscription had indeed been waiting for a week in his pigeon-hole, and he hurried off to get it.

The letter, enclosed in a thick envelope of azure cream-laid paper, sealed with aventurine wax, was written in that hand – angular down-strokes and cursive up-strokes – which denotes a high level of aristo-cratic education, and which young English ladies of good family all possess, a little too uniformly, perhaps.

This is what the letter, opened by M. d'Aspremont with a haste motivated perhaps by more than just curiosity, said:

My dear Mr Paul,

We have been in Naples for two months. During the journey, which we did in short stages, my uncle complained bitterly of the heat, the mosquitoes, the wine, the butter, and the beds; he swore that one must be completely mad to leave a comfortable cottage a few miles from London, and travel along dusty roads bordered by detestable inns, where not even your good old English dogs would consent to spend the night; but as he groused, he kept me company, and I would have taken him to the ends of the earth; he is none the worse for it and I am much better.

We are staying on the coast, in a whitewashed house buried in a sort of virgin forest of orange trees, lemon trees, myrtles, oleanders and other kind of exotic vegetation. From the terrace we enjoy a marvellous view, and every evening you will find a cup of tea ready for you here, or an iced lemonade, whichever you prefer. My uncle, whom you managed to fascinate, I don't know how, will be delighted to shake your hand. Need I add that your maidservant will not be annoyed either, although you cut her fingers with your ring, when bidding her farewell on the jetty at Folkestone?

Alicia W.

CHAPTER TWO

Paul d'Aspremont had dinner served for himself and then asked for a calash. There are always some of these parked around the big hotels, awaiting the whim of the travellers; so Paul's wish was granted there and then. Neapolitan hire horses are so skinny that they make Rocinante[5] seem positively overweight in comparison; their emaciated heads, their ribs sticking out like the hoops of barrels, their knobbly spines prominent and always grazed raw, seem to be pleading for the knacker's knife to put them out of their misery, for giving food to animals is viewed as a superfluous kindness in the careless south; the harnesses, as often as not broken, are supplemented by pieces of rope, and when the coachman has gathered his reins and clicked his tongue to get them going, you'd think the horses were going to faint away and the carriage vanish in a puff of smoke like Cinderella's coach when she returns home from the ball after the stroke of midnight, disobeying her good fairy's orders. But none of this actually happens; the nags brace themselves on their tottering legs and, after briefly staggering this way and that, break into a gallop from which they never falter: the coachman communicates his own ardour to them, and with a flick of his whip manages to bring out the last spark of life hidden in those carcasses. Pawing the ground, shaking their heads, giving themselves the airs of dashing steeds, rolling their eyes, flaring their nostrils, they keep going at a speed that the fastest English horse would not be able to keep up with. How is this phenomenon accomplished, and what power enables dead beasts to gallop along flat out? That's something we're not going to explain. The fact remains that this miracle occurs on a daily basis in Naples, and nobody there shows the slightest surprise.

M. Paul d'Aspremont's calash hurtled through the dense crowds, grazing the shops of the *acquaioli*[6] with their garlands of lemons, the open-air fried food and macaroni stalls, the displays of seafood and the heaps of watermelons piled up on the highway like cannon-balls in artillery parks. The *lazzaroni* sprawling at the foot of the walls, wrapped in their pea-jackets, barely deigned to draw in their legs so as not to have them driven over by the carriage; now and again, a *curricolo*[7], speeding along between its great scarlet wheels, passed by packed with a cargo of monks, nursemaids, *facchini* and assorted scamps, alongside the calash whose axle it grazed in the midst of a cloud of dust and noise. *Corricoli* are banned now, and it is forbidden to manufacture them any more; but you can always put a new body on old wheels, or new wheels on an old body – an ingenious means of allowing those strange vehicles to live on, to the great satisfaction of connoisseurs of local colour.

Our traveller paid only a distracted attention to this animated and picturesque spectacle which would certainly have absorbed any tourist who had not found at the hotel Roma a note addressed to him and signed Alicia W.

He gazed vacantly at the limpid blue sea, on which could be made out in the dazzling light – their outlines swathed at this distance in hues of amethyst and sapphire – the lovely islands that spread out fan-wise at the entrance to the gulf, Capri, Ischia, Nisida, Procida, their melodious names sounding like Greek dactyls: but his mind wasn't on them; it was winging its way towards Sorrento, and the little white house buried among the green trees and shrubs which Alicia's letter referred to. At this moment M. d'Aspremont's face did not have that indefinably off-putting expression which characterised it when an inner joy did not bring its disparate perfections harmoniously together: it was really handsome and *simpatico*, to use a word the Italians are fond of; the curve of his eyebrows was relaxed; the corners of his mouth were not bent disdainfully downwards, and a tender light was shining in his calm eyes; if you had seen him at the time, you would have perfectly well understood the feelings that seemed to be indicated by the half-tender, half-mocking phrases written about him on the cream-laid paper. His eccentricity, reinforced by his considerable distinction, was tailor-made to please a young miss, liberally brought up in the English style by a doting old uncle.

Given the speed at which the coachman was urging on his beasts, they would soon have shot past Chiaia and La Marinella; the calash drove through the countryside along that road that today has been replaced by a railway. A black dust, similar to crushed coal, gives a Plutonian appearance to that whole beach canopied by a dazzling sky and lapped by a sea of the sweetest blue; soot from Vesuvius, filtered by

11

the wind, sprinkles the shoreline, making the houses of Portici and Torre del Greco look like Birmingham factories. M. d'Aspremont wasn't in the slightest bit concerned by the contrast between the ebony earth and the sapphire sky, he was longing to reach his destination. The loveliest roads seem long when Miss Alicia is waiting for you at the end of them, and when you last said goodbye to each other six months ago on the pier at Folkestone: under such circumstances the sky and the sea of Naples lose their magic.

The calash left the main road, turned onto a track and stopped in front of a door formed by two pillars of white bricks, topped by urns of red clay, in which blossoming aloe flowers spread out their leaves, similar to sheets of tin plate and pointed like daggers. An openwork fence, painted green, served as a gate. Instead of a wall there was a cactus hedge whose shoots twisted themselves into irregular patterns and wove their sharp-pointed prickly pears into an inextricable tangle.

Above the hedge, three or four huge fig trees displayed the compact masses of their broad leaves of metallic green, with all the vigour of African vegetation; a large parasol pine was swaying its branches and the eye could barely make out, between the gaps in this luxuriant growth of foliage, the façade of the house shining in white patches through this thick bushy curtain.

A sunburnt servant woman with frizzy hair that was so thick a comb dragged through it would have snapped, ran up at the sound of the coach, opened the fence gate and, walking ahead of M. d'Aspremont along a path of laurel-roses whose branches stroked his cheek with their flowers, led him to the terrace where Miss Alicia was taking tea in the company of her uncle.

By a whim that perfectly suited a young woman jaded by all the comforts and elegances of life, and perhaps also to vex her uncle, whose middle-class tastes she mocked, Miss Alicia had chosen, in preference to more civilised dwelling-places, this villa whose owners were away on their travels and which had remained uninhabited for several years. She found in this abandoned garden that had almost reverted to the state of nature a wild poetry that gave her pleasure; in the active climate of Naples, everything in it had grown with prodigious vitality. Orange trees, myrtles, pomegranate trees and lemon trees had bloomed to their hearts' content, and their branches, having nothing more to fear from the knife of the pruner, reached out their hands to one another along the length of the path, or with easy familiarity poked into the bedrooms through a broken window-pane. There was nothing here of the melancholy of a deserted house, as in the north, but the reckless gaiety and cheerful petulance of nature, as found in the south, when left to its own devices; in the absence of a master the exuberant vegetation indulged itself in a joyful debauch of leaves, flowers, fruits and scents; they were taking back the place that mankind tries to deny them.

When the commodore – this was the familiar name by which Alicia called her uncle – saw this impenetrable thicket, which you would have needed a broad blade of the type used to fell trees to fight your way through, as in the forests of America, he protested loudly and decided that his niece was definitely mad. But Alicia gravely promised him that she would have a passage made from the main door to the living-room, and from the living-room to the terrace, big enough for a barrel of malmsey to get through – the only concession she was prepared to make to her uncle's enlightened spirit. The commodore resignedly agreed, for he was unable to resist his niece, and just now, sitting opposite her on the terrace, he was sipping, disguised as tea, a big cup full of rum.

This terrace, which had been the main attraction as far as the young miss was concerned, was indeed really very picturesque, and deserves a description all to itself, for Paul d'Aspremont will be returning here frequently, and one should paint the stage setting of the scenes one is narrating.

You climbed onto this terrace, whose sheer vertical sides overlooked a sunken path, up steps made of broad disjointed flagstones between which flourished tenacious weeds. Four weather-beaten columns, taken from some ancient ruin, their lost capitals replaced by stone dice, supported a trellis of poles entwined and roofed over by vines. From the parapets there hung thick streamers and garlands of wild vines and wall-plants. At the foot of the walls, Indian figs, aloes, and arbutus trees grew in charming disorder, and beyond a wood dominated by a palm tree and three Italian pines, the view extended across the rolling terrain dotted with white villas, and came to rest on the purplish silhouette of

Vesuvius, or lost itself in the blue immensity of the sea.

When M. Paul d'Aspremont appeared on the topmost step, Alicia got up, uttered a short cry of joy and went up to meet him. Paul took her hand, English-style, but the young woman lifted her captive hand to her friend's lips with a movement full of childish affection and innocent coquettishness.

The commodore tried to get up on his somewhat gouty legs, and finally managed it after a few attempts which had him grimacing with pain, an expression that contrasted comically with the look of jubilation spread out on his broad, beaming face; with steps that were quite assured for him, he came up to the charming group formed by the two young people, and shook Paul's hand in such a pincer-grip that he almost crushed his fingers together, which is the supreme expression of old-fashioned British cordiality.

Miss Alicia Ward belonged to that variety of English brunettes who are the realisation of an ideal whose preconditions seem to contradict one another: a skin so dazzlingly white that it makes milk, snow, lilies, alabaster, virgin wax, and everything that poets use in their similes of whiteness look yellow in comparison; lips of cherry, and hair as black as night on a raven's wing. The effect of this sharp contrast is irresistible and produces a kind of beauty apart, for which there is no equivalent anywhere else. Perhaps a few Circassian women brought up from childhood in the seraglio present the same miraculous complexion, but for this we have to take on trust the exaggerations of oriental poetry and the watercolours of Lewis[8] depicting the harems of Cairo. Alicia was assuredly the most perfect type of this kind of beauty.

The lengthened oval of her head, her complexion of incomparable beauty, her fine, slender nose, her dark blue eyes fringed with long lashes which fluttered on her rosy cheeks like black butterflies when she batted her eyelids, her lips gleaming bright crimson, her hair falling in shining coils like satin ribbons on either side of her cheeks and her swan's neck, bore witness to the truth of those romantic portraits of women by Maclise[9] which, at the Universal Exhibition, seemed to be charming impostures.

Alicia was wearing a dress of grenadine with flounces festooned and embroidered with red palmettes, which went marvellously with the small-grained coral braids that made up her coiffure, her necklace and her bracelets; five pendant stones hanging from a multifaceted coral pearl trembled at the lobes of her small and delicately curled ears. – If you disapprove of this misuse of coral, remember that we are in Naples, and that fishermen come up out of the sea with the express intention of presenting you with those coral branches that turn red when exposed to air.

We owe it to you, after the portrait of Miss Alicia Ward, and if only to present a contrast with it, to give you at the very least a caricature of the commodore, in the style of Hogarth.

The commodore, a man of sixty-something, had the peculiarity of displaying a face of uniformly flaming crimson, on which his white eyebrows and mutton-chop whiskers of the same colour stood out, making him look like an old redskin who has tattooed himself with chalk. Exposure to the blazing sun, an inseparable corollary of travelling through Italy, had added a few more layers to this fiery colouring, and the commodore couldn't help but make you think of a chocolate praline wrapped in cotton wool. He was dressed from head to toe – jacket, waistcoat, trousers and gaiters – in a sturdy purplish-grey material, which his tailor must have sworn on his honour was the most fashionable and elegant hue, an assertion which may well have been true. Despite this gleaming complexion and this grotesque outfit, the commodore in no way looked vulgar. His painstaking cleanliness, his irreproachable bearing and his lordly manners were all signs of the perfect gentleman, although he bore more than a superficial likeness to vaudeville Englishmen as parodied by Hoffmann or Levassor. His character consisted in worshipping his niece and drinking plenty of port and Jamaica rum to keep up his level of damp radicals, following the method of Corporal Trim.

'Just look how well I am now, and how beautiful! Look at the colour in my cheeks – not as ruddy as my uncle's, yet; and that won't ever be the case, I hope! – But here there's a trace of pink, real pink,' said Alicia drawing across her cheek her slender finger with, at its tip, a fingernail shining like agate; 'I've put on weight too, and no one can see those poor little salt-cellar collarbones that I used to hate so much when I went to the ball. Tell me, what a coquette a girl must be to deprive herself of her fiancé's company for three months, so that after that period of absence he can find her looking fresh and splendid!'

And as she came out with this tirade, in the bantering and frisky tone characteristic of her, Alicia was standing in front of Paul as if to provoke him almost challengingly to look her over.

'She's quite right,' added the commodore; 'don't you think she's looking sturdy now and as splendid as those girls from Procida who carry Greek amphoras on their heads?'

'That's quite true, commodore,' replied Paul; 'Miss Alicia hasn't grown any more beautiful, that would be impossible, but it's obvious that she's in better health than when, out of coquetry – or so she claims – she imposed this painful separation on me.'

And his eyes rested in a strange fixed stare on the young woman standing before him.

Suddenly the pretty pink flush that she had boasted of having lured to her face disappeared from Alicia's cheeks, as the russet tones of evening leave the snowy cheeks of the mountainside when the sun dips below the horizon; trembling all over, she clutched her heart; her charming lips, grown pallid, tightened.

Paul stood up in alarm, as did the commodore; Alicia's vivid colours had reappeared; she smiled with some effort.

'I promised you a cup of tea or a sorbet; although I'm English, I'd recommend the sorbet. Snow is better than hot water in this country that's next to Africa, from where the sirocco arrives in a direct line.'

All three took their seats around the stone table, beneath the canopy of vines; the sun had dived into the sea, and the blue day that in Naples is called night had succeeded the yellow day. The moon was scattering silver coins on the terrace through the jagged gaps in the foliage; the sea was swooshing against the shore like a kiss, and in the distance you could hear the coppery ripple of tambourines accompanying the tarantellas…

It was time to separate. Vicè, the tawny servant woman with frizzy hair, came with a lantern to take Paul back through the maze of the garden. While serving the sorbets and the iced water, she had gazed at the newcomer with an expression of mingled curiosity and fear. Doubtless, the result of her scrutiny had not been in Paul's favour, as

Vicè's brow, already as yellow-brown as a cigar, had grown even darker; and as she saw off the stranger, she pointed at him, without him being able to see, the little finger and index finger of her hand, while the other two fingers, bent back against the palm, joined her thumb as if to form a cabalistic sign.

CHAPTER THREE

Alicia's friend returned to the hotel Roma by the same road: the late evening was incomparably beautiful; a clear, shining moon shed across the diaphanous blue water a long trail of silver spangles whose perpetual shimmering, caused by the lapping of the waves, multiplied its gleam. Out at sea, the fishermen's boats, carrying at their prow an iron lantern filled with flaming oakum, dotted the sea with red stars and left scarlet trails in their wake; the smoke from Vesuvius, white in the daytime, had changed into a glowing pillar that also cast its reflection across the gulf. At this moment the bay was showing the appearance, so improbable to northern eyes, which it assumes in those black-framed Italian watercolours that were so common a few years ago, and are more faithful in their crude exaggeration than people think.

A few *lazzaroni* out for a night stroll were still wandering along the shore, unconsciously moved by this magical spectacle, and allowing their big black eyes to lose themselves in the bluish expanse. Others, sitting on the plank of a foundered fishing boat, were singing an aria from *Lucia*, or else the popular love song in vogue at the time: '*Te voglio ben' assai*',[10] in voices that would have been the envy of many a tenor with an earning power of a hundred thousand francs. Naples stays up late, like all cities in the south; but the lights from the windows were extinguished one by one, and only the lottery kiosks, with their garlands of coloured paper, their favourite numbers, and the gleam of their lanterns were still open, ready to accept the money of those whimsical gamblers susceptible to the temptation, as they made their way home, of placing a few *carlini* or a few ducats[11] on a number that had come to them in their dreams.

Paul went to bed, drew round him the gauze curtains of the mosquito net, and was soon asleep. As happens to travellers who have just made a sea crossing, his bed, although motionless, seemed to him to be pitching and rolling, as if the hotel Roma had been the *Leopold*. This impression made him dream that he was still at sea and that he could see, on the jetty, Alicia looking very pale, standing next to her crimson-faced uncle and waving at him not to land; the young woman's face was filled with an expression of deep distress, and by thus warding him off she seemed to be obeying, against her will, some imperious destiny.

This dream, which derived its extreme sense of reality from images that were still recent, caused the sleeper so much sorrow that he awoke, and he was happy to find himself back in his bedroom, where there flickered, with an opal glimmer, a night-light shedding its gleam on a small porcelain tower besieged by buzzing mosquitoes. So as not to relapse into that painful dream, Paul fought off sleep and started to recall the beginnings of his relationship with Miss Alicia, going over one by one all those childishly delightful scenes of first love.

In his mind's eye he saw the red-brick house, surrounded by wild roses and honeysuckle, where Miss Alicia lived in Richmond with her uncle, and to which, on his first visit to England, he had been introduced by one of those letters of recommendation whose effect is usually limited to an invitation to dinner. He remembered the white dress of Indian muslin, set off by a simple ribbon, which Alicia, who had left her boarding-school the day before, was wearing on that particular occasion, and the branch of jasmine that unfurled across the cascade of her hair like a flower from the crown of Ophelia when she is swept away by the current; he remembered her velvet-blue eyes, and her half-opened mouth, giving a glimpse of her little pearly teeth, and her frail neck which stretched out like that of an attentive bird, and her sudden blushes when the eyes of the young French gentleman met hers.

The parlour with its brown panelling and its green drapes, decorated with engravings showing fox-hunts and steeplechases coloured in the vivid tones of English illustrations, reproduced its image in his brain as if in a camera obscura. The piano's row of keys stretched out like a dowager's teeth. The mantelpiece, festooned with a twig of Irish ivy, imparted a glow to its cast-iron shell polished with graphite; the oak armchairs resting on carved feet opened their arms upholstered in morocco leather, the carpet spread out its rosettes, and Miss Alicia, trembling like a leaf, sang in the most adorably out-of-key voice in the world the romance from *Anna Bolena*, '*Deh! non voler costringere*',[12] which Paul, no less moved but unable to keep time, accompanied at the piano, while the commodore, made drowsy by a laborious digestion and even more crimson than usual, let slip to the ground a colossal copy of *The Times*, with its supplement.

Then the scene changed: Paul, now on more intimate terms, had been invited by the commodore to spend a few days at his cottage in Lincolnshire... An old feudal castle, with crenellated towers and Gothic windows, half enveloped in an immense growth of ivy, but arranged indoors with all modern comforts, rose up at the end of a lawn whose ray-grass, carefully watered and tamped down, was as smooth as velvet; a path of yellow sand curved round the lawn and acted as a riding ring for Miss Alicia, mounted on one of those Scottish ponies with dishevelled manes that Sir Edward Landseer likes to paint, and to which he gives an almost human expression. Paul, on a cherry-bay horse that the commodore had lent him, accompanied Miss Ward in her circular trots, for the doctor, who had found her a little weak in the chest, had ordered her to take exercise.

On another occasion a light boat glided across the pond, shouldering aside the water lilies and sending a kingfisher flying away under the silvery foliage of the willows. It was Alicia who rowed and Paul who took the helm; how pretty she was in the golden halo of the straw hat round her head, as the sun's rays shone through it! She would lean backwards to pull on the oar; the polished tip of her grey ankle-boot rested on the wooden seat; Miss Ward didn't have those Andalucian feet, all stubby and round like domestic irons, that are admired in Spain; her ankle was slender, her instep nicely arched, and the soles of her boots, a little on the long side perhaps, were less than an inch thick.

The commodore remained 'chained' to the shore, not out of a sense of hauteur, but because of his weight, which would have made the frail craft and its crew sink; he waited for his niece at the landing stage, and with maternal solicitude threw a mantelet over her shoulders so she wouldn't catch cold, then the boat was moored to its peg, and they returned for lunch in the house. It was a pleasure to see how Alicia, who ordinarily ate as little as a bird, tore with her pearly teeth into a pink slice of paper-thin York ham, and nibbled a bread roll without leaving a single crumb for the goldfish in the pond.

Happy days pass so quickly! Paul kept putting off his departure from week to week, and the fine clumps of foliage in the park were starting to put on their saffron-yellow hues; white mists rose in the mornings from the pond. Despite the perpetual scraping of the gardener's rake, dead leaves were strewn across the sand of the path; millions of little frozen pearls glittered on the greensward of the lawn, and in the evenings you could see the magpies hopping about and quarrelling among the topmost branches of the bare trees.

Alicia was growing paler even as Paul's eyes rested anxiously on her, and the only colour she preserved was two small pink patches above her cheek-bones. She was often cold, and the hottest of coal fires wasn't enough to warm her. The doctor had seemed worried, and his last prescription recommended Miss Ward to spend the winter in Pisa and the summer in Naples.

Family business had recalled Paul to France; Alicia and the commodore were to leave for Italy, and they had parted at Folkestone. Not a word had been uttered, but Miss Ward viewed Paul as her fiancé, and the commodore had given the young man a significantly forceful handshake: you only crush a son-in-law's fingers like that.

Paul, his next meeting with her adjourned for six months – as long as six centuries for his impatient spirit – had been fortunate to find Alicia cured of her lassitude and radiant with health. Anything still childlike about the young woman had disappeared; and he was exhilarated at the thought that the commodore would have no objection when he finally asked for his niece's hand in marriage.

Lulled by these pleasant images, he went back to sleep and awoke when it was already daylight. Naples' hullabaloo had already begun; the iced-water vendors were crying their wares; sellers of roast meat were offering passers-by their hunks of meat threaded on skewers; leaning from their windows, lazy housewives were lowering down on pieces of string their shopping baskets which they then hauled up again, loaded with tomatoes, fish, and great quarters of pumpkin. The public writers, in threadbare black coats and pens stuck behind their ears, sat at their stalls; the money-changers laid out on their tables piles of *grani*, *carlini* and ducats; the coachmen set their old nags galloping off in search of their morning fares, and the bells in every church tower joyfully pealed out the Angelus.

Our traveller, wrapped in his dressing-gown, leant on his elbows at the balcony; from the window one could see Santa Lucia, the Castel dell'Ovo, and an immense stretch of sea as far as Vesuvius and the blue promontory where the vast *casini* of Castellammare gleamed white, and in the distance the villas of Sorrento were just visible.

The sky was clear; just one light, white cloud was moving towards the city, blown along by a nonchalant breeze. Paul fixed his eyes on it with that strange stare we have already noticed; he frowned. Other vaporous clouds came to join that solitary wisp, and soon a thick curtain of clouds spread its dark folds over the Castel Sant'Elmo. Large drops of rain fell onto the lava paving, and in a few minutes turned into one of those downpours which transform the streets of Naples into so many torrents and sweep away dogs and even donkeys into the sewers. The crowd, taken by surprise, scattered, looking for shelter; the open-air shops hastily packed up and made a run for it, losing part of their wares in the process, and the rain, now victoriously bestriding the battlefield, swept in white gusts across the deserted quay of Santa Lucia.

The gigantic *facchino* on whom Paddy had landed such an adroit punch, leaning against a wall under a jutting balcony which gave him some protection, had not let himself be carried away in the general rout, and was directing a profoundly meditative gaze at the window where M. Paul d'Aspremont was leaning.

His inner monologue could be summarised in this phrase, which he grumbled angrily:

'The captain of the *Leopold* would have done well to chuck that *forestiere*[13] overboard'; and, reaching his hand through the opening in his great canvas shirt, he touched the bundle of amulets on a piece of ribbon hanging round his neck.

CHAPTER FOUR

The fine weather had returned in no time at all, a bright ray of sunshine dried up in a few minutes the last tears of the shower, and the crowd started once more to swarm merrily along the quay. But Timberio, the porter, seemed still to be of the same mind regarding the young French stranger, and he prudently transported his penates out of sight of the hotel windows: a few *lazzaroni* of his acquaintance manifested their surprise that he was abandoning an excellent spot to choose one that was much less favourable.

'I'll give it to anyone who wants to take it,' he replied, nodding with an air of mystery; 'I know what I know.'

Paul had breakfast in his room since, either out of timidity or disdain, he didn't like finding himself surrounded by people; then he dressed, and while waiting for a suitable time at which to go over to Miss Ward's, he visited the museum of the Studii: he absent-mindedly admired the precious collection of Campanian vases, the bronzes found in the excavations at Pompeii, the bronze Greek helmet covered in verdigris still containing the head of the soldier who had been wearing it, the chunk of solidified mud preserving, like a mould, the imprint of the charming torso of a young woman whom the eruption had caught in the country house of Arrius Diomedes, the Farnese Hercules and his prodigious set of muscles, the Flora, the archaic Minerva, the two Balbuses, and the magnificent statue of Aristides, perhaps the most perfect work that the ancient world has left us. But a man in love is not going to show a particularly enthusiastic appreciation of artistic monuments; for him, the slightest sidelong glimpse of his beloved's head is worth all the Greek or Roman marbles in the world.

Having succeeded in spinning out as well as he could two or three hours in the Studii, he jumped into his calash and headed out to the country house where Miss Ward was staying. The coachman, with that understanding of the passions which characterises southern natures, urged his nags on at top speed, and soon the coach stopped in front of the pillars topped with luxuriant plants that we have already described. The same servant woman came to half-open the openwork gate in the fence; her hair still twisted and turned in rebellious curls; all she was wearing, like the first time, was a shirt of coarse canvas, embroidered on the sleeves and at the collar by trimmings of coloured thread, and a thick fabric skirt with transverse multicoloured stripes, of the kind worn by the women of Procida; her legs, we have to confess, were bare of stockings, and she placed in the dust naked feet that would have attracted the admiration of a sculptor. But from a black ribbon hung on her breast a bundle of little odd-shaped charms in horn and coral, on which, to Vicè's evident satisfaction, Paul's gaze rested.

Miss Alicia was out on the terrace, her favourite part of the house. An Indian hammock of red and white, decorated with birds' feathers, hanging from two of the columns which supported the roof of vines, swung the young woman nonchalantly to and fro; she was wrapped in a light peignoir of raw China silk, whose fluted trimmings she was mercilessly allowing to get crumpled. Her feet, the tips of which could be seen through the mesh of the hammock, were shod in aloe-fibre slippers, and her beautiful bare arms were folded above and behind her head, in the attitude of the Cleopatra of antiquity, for although it was still only the beginning of May, the heat was already extreme, and thousands of cicadas were shrilling in chorus from beneath the bushes all around.

The commodore, dressed like a planter and sitting on a rush armchair, pulled at regular intervals the cord which kept the hammock swaying.

A third person completed the group; it was Count Altavilla, a young Neapolitan man-about-town whose presence brought to Paul's brow that contraction which gave his physiognomy an expression of diabolical malevolence.

The Count was, indeed, one of those men whom one doesn't like to see too close to a woman one loves. He was tall and perfectly proportioned; his hair was jet-black, swept up into abundant tufts over his smooth and finely sculptured forehead; a gleam of Naples' sunshine sparkled in his eyes, and his teeth, broad and strong and yet as pure as pearls, seemed to be even more dazzling because of the bright red of his lips and the olive hue of his complexion. The only criticism a meticulous taste might have found to make against the Count was that he was just too handsome.

As for his clothes, Altavilla had them brought over from London, and even the most severe dandy would have approved of his outfit. In his whole costume the only thing that seemed Italian was his excessively expensive shirt buttons. Here, the child of the south's perfectly natural liking for jewellery gave itself away. Perhaps, too, anywhere other than in Naples you might have noted as being in rather middling taste the group of objects that were hanging from a single ring of his watch-chain: a sheaf of forking coral branches, hands shaped in the lava of Vesuvius with fingers folded or brandishing a dagger, dogs stretching out on their paws, black and white pieces of horn, and other similar small items; but a quick walk along the Via Toledo or the Villa Reale would have been enough to demonstrate that the Count was not being particularly eccentric in wearing on his waistcoat these bizarre lucky charms.

When Paul d'Aspremont presented himself, the Count, at Miss Ward's insistence, was singing one of those delightful popular Neapolitan melodies, with no known author, any one of which, taken down by a musician, would be enough to make the fortune of an opera. If you have never heard these songs, on the Chiaia shore or out on the pier, coming from the mouth of a *lazzarone*, a fisherman or a *trovatella*, the charming romances of Gordigiani will give you some idea of them.[14] They are a mixture of a sighing breeze, a ray of moonlight, the perfume of an orange tree and the beating of a heart.

Alicia, with her pretty, slightly off-key English voice, was following the tune which she wanted to try and memorise, and as she continued she gave a friendly little wave to Paul, who was watching her with a less than amiable expression, irritated by the presence of this handsome young man.

One of the cords of the hammock snapped, and Miss Ward slid onto the ground, but without hurting herself; six hands reached out simultaneously to help her. The young woman was already on her feet, flushed pink all over with embarrassment, since it is quite 'improper' to fall down in front of gentlemen. However, not a single one of the chaste folds in her dress had been put out of place.

'I'd tested those cords myself, you know,' said the commodore, 'and Miss Ward weighs hardly any more than a hummingbird.'

Count Altavilla nodded with a mysterious expression on his face: he obviously had his own private explanation for the cord's snapping, and it wasn't a question of weight; but, as a well-brought-up man, he kept his silence, and contented himself with fiddling with the bunch of lucky charms on his waistcoat.

Like all men who, when they find themselves in the presence of someone they consider a potentially dangerous rival, become sullen and unsociable instead of being twice as graceful and amiable, Paul d'Aspremont, although an experienced man of the world, did not succeed in hiding his ill humour; he replied only in monosyllables, let the conversation languish, and when his gaze turned to Altavilla, it took on its sinister look; the yellow fibrils twisted and turned behind the grey transparency of his eyes, like water snakes in the depths of a stream.

Each time Paul looked at him like that, the Count, with an apparently mechanical gesture, would tear a flower from the window-box at his side and throw it away as if to cut through the angry beam of that gaze.

'Why are you laying waste to my garden like that?' exclaimed Miss Ward, when she noticed this gesture. 'What have my flowers done against you for you to decapitate them?'

'Oh, nothing, miss! It's just a nervous tic,' replied Altavilla, cutting off with his fingernail a superb rose that he threw down to join the rest.

'You're getting on my nerves in the most horrid way,' said Alicia; 'and without meaning to, you're falling foul of one of my quirks. I've never picked a flower. A bouquet fills me with a sort of dread: for it is made of dead flowers, the corpses of roses, verbenas or periwinkles, whose fragrance seems to me to have a whiff of the tomb about it.'

'To expiate the murders I have just committed,' said Count Altavilla with a bow, 'I will send you a hundred baskets of living flowers.'

Paul had stood up, and, looking strained, was twiddling the edge of his hat like someone planning an imminent exit.

'What's this? Are you leaving already?' said Miss Ward.

'I've got some letters to write, important letters.'

'Oh! what a nasty thing to say!' said the young woman, with a little pout. 'Can any letters be important when you're not writing them to me?'

'Do stay, Paul,' said the commodore; 'I'd been mentally planning things out for the evening, depending on my niece's approval: we would have gone first to drink a glass of water from the fountain of Santa Lucia – it smells of rotten eggs, but gives you an appetite; we'd have eaten one or two dozen oysters, white and red ones, at the fish stall, dined under a trellis in some authentic Neapolitan *osteria*, drunk some Falerno and Lacrima Christi, and ended the entertainment with a visit to Signor Pulcinella[15]. The Count would have explained to us the subtleties of his dialect.'

This plan seemed to hold few charms for M. d'Aspremont, and he withdrew after a frigid bow.

Altavilla remained a few moments longer; and as Miss Ward, cross at Paul's departure, was disinclined to go along with the commodore's plans, he took his leave.

Two hours later, Miss Alicia received an immense number of flower-pots, containing the rarest flowers, and, what surprised her even more, a monstrous pair of the horns of a Sicilian ox, as transparent as jasper, as polished as agate, measuring a good three feet long and ending in menacing sharp black tips. A magnificent gilt bronze mounting enabled one to place the horns, point upwards, on a mantelpiece, a sideboard, or a cornice.

Vicè, who had helped the porters to unpack the flowers and horns, seemed to understand the significance of this strange present.

She placed in full view, on a stone table, the superb crescent-shaped horns, which looked as if they had been pulled from the brow of the superb bull who bore off Europa, and said, 'Now we're able to defend ourselves.'

'What do you mean, Vicè?' asked Miss Ward.

'Nothing… it's just that the French signore has very strange eyes.'

CHAPTER FIVE

Mealtime had long since gone by, and the embers of the coal fires which during the day transformed the kitchen of the hotel Roma into the crater of Vesuvius were slowly dying down under the sheet-metal dampers; the pots and pans had resumed their positions on their respective nails and were shining all in a row like shields along the plank of an ancient trireme; a yellow copper lamp, similar to those that are dug up in the excavations at Pompeii, hanging by a triple chain from the main beam of the ceiling, illuminated with its three wicks artlessly dipping into oil the centre of the vast kitchen whose corners were immersed in shadow.

The bright rays falling from above seemed to mould, with their picturesque play of light and shade, a group of characteristic figures gathered around the bulky wooden table, scored and furrowed by cook's knives across its whole surface, that occupied the middle of this big room where the smoke from culinary activities had glazed the walls with that bitumen so dear to painters of the school of Caravaggio. To be sure, José Ribera or Salvator Rosa, in their robust love of the real, would not have disdained the models gathered there by chance – or, to be more precise, brought together by habit as they were each evening.

First there was the chef, Virgilio Falsacappa, a highly important person, colossal in stature and formidable in girth, who might have been mistaken for one of Vitellius' guests[16] if, instead of a white cotton damask jacket, he had been wearing a Roman toga trimmed with scarlet: his prodigiously sharply defined features formed as it were a kind of solemn caricature of certain types of ancient medals; thick black beetling eyebrows, half an inch in length, crowned his eyes that were cut out of his face like those in theatre masks; an enormous nose threw its shadow on his wide mouth that seemed furnished with three rows of teeth like a shark's jaws. A mighty dewlap like that of the Farnese bull extended from his chin, with a dimple deep enough to stick your fist in, to a neck of athletic vigour criss-crossed by veins and muscles. Two tufts of sideburns, each of which could have provided a sapper with a reasonable size of beard, framed that broad face hammered and beaten into violent colours: curly hair, gleaming black, in which a few silvery threads were mingled, twisted across his skull in short little locks, and the nape of his neck, creased by three horizontal swellings, hung over the collar of his jacket; on his earlobes, set off by the swelling jawbones capable of grinding their way through an ox in a single day, gleamed silver earrings as big as a full moon; such was master Virgilio Falsa-cappa, to whom his apron hiked up around his haunches and his knife thrust into a wooden sheath gave the appearance more of a ritual slaughterer than a cook.

Then there was Timberio the porter, whom the gymnastics of his profession and the sobriety of his régimen, which consisted of a handful of half-cooked macaroni sprinkled with *caciocavallo*[17], a slice of water-melon and a glass of iced water, maintained in a state of relative skinni-ness, and who, if well fed, would certainly have attained the girth of Falsacappa, so much did his robust frame seem made to support a huge weight of flesh. He was wearing nothing more than shorts, a long brown fabric waistcoat and a coarse pea-jacket slung across his shoulder.

Leaning against the edge of the table, Scazziga, the coachman of the hired calash used by M. Paul d'Aspremont, also cut a striking figure; his irregular, alert features were suffused with artless guile; a smile he could turn on or off lingered on his mocking lips, and you could see by the affability of his manners that he lived in perpetual proximity to the right sort of people; his clothes, purchased from the second-hand shop, simulated a kind of livery which he took no little pride in and which, in his mind, placed a great social distance between himself and the savage Timberio; his conversation was sprinkled with English and French words which didn't always tally very felicitously with the meaning of what he wanted to say, but which nonetheless aroused the admiration of the kitchen girls and the chef's assistants, astonished at such erudition.

Standing a little further back were two young servant girls whose features recalled, with less nobility no doubt, that type so familiar from Syracusan coins: a low forehead, a nose melding into the forehead, thickish lips, a strong, dumpy chin; hair bluish-black in colour, parted down the middle, and gathered behind their heads into a heavy bun held in place by pins with coral tips. Necklaces of the same material encircled in a triple row their caryatid necks, whose muscles had been strengthened by the habit of carrying burdens on their heads. Dandies would certainly have despised these poor girls who preserved, pure of any foreign admixture, the blood of the splendid races of Magna Graecia; but any artist, on seeing them, would have taken out his sketch-book and sharpened his pencil.

Have you ever seen, in the Marshal Soult gallery in the Louvre, the painting by Murillo where the cherubs are doing the cooking? If you have, that will dispense us from having to depict here the heads of the three or four curly- and frizzy-haired chef's assistants who completed the group.

They were deep in serious discussion. The topic was M. Paul d'Aspremont, the French traveller who had arrived on the last steamer: downstairs was making so bold as to judge upstairs.

It was the turn of Timberio the porter to speak, and he left a pause between each of his sentences, like a fashionable actor, to give his audience the time to seize its full import, and to grant assent or raise objections.

'Follow my argument closely,' the orator was saying; 'the *Leopold* is a decent Tuscan steamer, which one can have no objection to, except that it transports too many English heretics…'

'The English heretics pay good money,' interrupted Scazziga, made more tolerant by their generous tips.

'No doubt; it's the least a heretic can do, when he makes a proper Christian sweat for him: reward him generously, so as to lessen the humiliation.'

'I'm not humiliated at carrying a *forestiere* in my coach; I don't have to play the beast of burden like you, Timberio.'

'Aren't I baptised just as much as you?' replied the porter, frowning and clenching his fists.

'Let Timberio have his say,' the assembly chorused, afraid to see this interesting display of eloquence turn into a quarrel.

'You will grant me,' resumed the orator more calmly, 'that the weather was superb when the *Leopold* came into port?'

'We grant you as much, Timberio,' said the chef, with condescending majesty.

'The sea was as smooth as a mirror,' continued the *facchino*, 'and yet a huge wave shook Gennaro's boat so roughly that he fell into the water with two or three of his mates. Is it natural? Gennaro has his sea legs, after all, and he could dance a tarantella on a yard-arm without a balancing pole.'

'Perhaps he'd drunk one *fiasco* of Asprino too many,' objected Scazziga, the rationalist of the assembly.

'Not even a glass of lemonade,' continued Timberio; 'but on board the boat there was a gentleman looking at him in a certain way, you get my drift!'

'Oh, perfectly well!' they replied in chorus, all pointing their index and little fingers with admirable unanimity.

'And this gentleman,' said Timberio, 'was none other than Paul d'Aspremont.'

'The one lodging in number three,' asked the chef, 'the one whose dinner I send up on a tray?'

'Precisely,' replied the youngest and prettiest of the servant girls; 'I've never seen a more unsociable, more disagreeable and more disdainful traveller; he didn't give me a single glance, or a single word, and yet I'm worth a compliment, all the gentlemen say so.'

'You're worth more than that, Gelsomina my lovely,' said Timberio gallantly; 'but it's a good thing for you that this foreigner never noticed you.'

'You are much too superstitious as well,' objected the sceptical Scazziga, whose relations with foreigners had turned him into something of a Voltairean.

'If you go on rubbing shoulders with heretics you'll even end up disbelieving in San Gennaro[18].'

'If your Gennaro was so clumsy as to fall into the sea, that's no reason,' continued Scazziga, defending his client, 'to assume that M. Paul d'Aspremont has the influence you attribute to him.'

'You need other proofs? This morning I saw him at his window, his eyes fixed on a cloud no bigger than a feather drifting out of a pillow that's come unstitched, and straight away big black clouds gathered, and it rained so heavily the dogs could drink without having to dip their heads.'

Scazziga was not convinced and shook his head dubiously.

'And the groom's no better than the master,' continued Timberio; 'that monkey in boots must be in league with the devil for him to have thrown me to the ground, me that could kill him with a flick of my finger.'

'I agree with Timborio,' said the chef majestically; 'the foreigner doesn't eat much; he sent back the stuffed zucchini, the roast chicken and the tomato macaroni I had prepared with my own hands! Some strange secret is lurking under all that sobriety. Why would a wealthy man go without tasty dishes and make do with egg soup and a slice of cold meat?'

'He's a redhead,' said Gelsomina, raking her fingers through the black forest of her own hair.

'And he has protruding eyes,' continued Pepina, the other servant girl.

'Set very close together,' added Timberio.

'And the crease between his eyebrows makes the shape of a horseshoe,' said, as if to rest his case, the formidable Virgilio Falsacappa; 'so he must be…'

'Don't say it, there's no point!' they exclaimed in chorus, all except for Scazziga who was still unconvinced; 'we'll be on our guard.'

'When I think I'd be hassled by the police,' said Trimberio, 'if I just happened to drop a three-hundred-pound traveller's trunk on the head of that wretched *forestiere*!'

'Scazziga must be a brave fellow to drive him around,' said Gelsomina.

'I'm up on my seat, he can only see my back, and his eyes can't meet mine at the right angle. Anyway, a fat lot I care.'

'You have no religion, Scazziga,' said the colossal Palforio, the cook of Herculean proportions; 'you'll come to a sticky end.'

While they were thus holding forth about him at the hotel Roma, Paul, who had been put into a bad mood by the presence of Count Altavilla at Miss Ward's, had gone out for a stroll by the Villa Reale; and more than once the crease on his brow grew furrowed, and his eyes assumed their fixed stare. He thought he saw Alicia passing by in a calash with the Count and the commodore, and he rushed over to the carriage window, placing his pince-nez on his nose to make sure he wasn't mistaken: it wasn't Alicia, but a woman who from a distance looked rather like her. But the horses of the calash, doubtless startled by Paul's sudden movement, galloped off.

Paul had an ice-cream at the café Europa on the largo of the palace: several people examined him curiously, and changed places, making a strange gesture.

He went into the Pulcinella theatre, where they were putting on a *tutto da ridere*[19] show. The actor stumbled in the middle of his farcical improvisation, and dried up; he tried again; but right in the middle of his *lazzi*, his black cardboard nose came loose, and he couldn't manage to stick it back on again; and as if to excuse himself, he explained his misadventures by making a quick gesture, for Paul's stare, resting on him, deprived him of all his faculties.

The spectators near Paul slipped away one by one; M. d'Aspremont rose to leave, unaware of the strange effect he was producing, and in the corridor he heard people muttering this strange word, quite without meaning for him: '*Jettatore! jettatore!*'[20]

CHAPTER SIX

The day after the dispatch of the horns, Count Altavilla came to call on Miss Ward. The young Englishwoman was taking tea in the company of her uncle, exactly as if she had been in Ramsgate in a house of yellow bricks, and not in Naples on a whitewashed terrace surrounded by fig trees, cactuses and aloe trees; for one of the characteristic signs of the Saxon race is the way it keeps up its habits, however contrary to the climate they may be. The commodore was beaming; by means of pieces of ice that he had manufactured chemically with an apparatus – for only snow is brought down from the mountains rising behind Castellammare – he had managed to keep his butter from melting, and he was spreading a layer of it with visible satisfaction across a slice of bread cut to make a sandwich.

After those few vague words which precede any conversation and resemble the preludes with which pianists test out their keyboard before starting to perform their piece, Alicia, suddenly abandoning the usual commonplace remarks, all at once addressed the young Neapolitan count:

'What is the meaning of that strange gift of horns which accompanied your flowers? My servant Vicè told me it was a protection against the *fascino*; but that was all I could get out of her.'

'Vicè is correct,' replied the Count, with a bow.

'But what is the *fascino*?' pressed the young girl; 'I'm not well informed about your… African superstitions, for it is all connected, no doubt, with some popular belief.'

'The *fascino* is the pernicious influence exerted by the person gifted, or rather afflicted, with the evil eye.'

'I'll pretend to understand you, for fear of giving you an unfavourable idea of my intelligence by confessing that the sense of your words eludes me,' said Miss Alicia Ward. 'You're explaining one unknown by another: evil eye is a very poor translation, as far as I am concerned, for *fascino*; like the character in the comedy, I know Latin – but please just pretend I don't.'

'I will explain it to you with all possible clarity,' replied Altavilla; 'but in your British disdain, don't start taking me for a savage, and wondering whether my clothes might not hide a skin tattooed in red and blue. I'm a civilised man; I was brought up in Paris, I speak English and French; I've read Voltaire; I believe in steamboats, in railways, and in the two chambers, like Stendhal; I eat macaroni with a fork; in the morning I wear suede gloves, in the afternoon dyed gloves, in the evening straw-yellow gloves.'

The attention of the commodore, who was buttering his second slice of bread, was captured by this strange beginning, and he froze, knife in hand, fixing on Altavilla his polar-blue eyes, the colour of which contrasted strangely with his brick-red complexion.

'Those are reassuring qualifications,' said Miss Alicia with a smile; 'and after that I would need to be quite lacking in trust to suspect you of *barbarity*. But is what you have to tell me so very terrible or absurd if you have to employ so many circumlocutions to get to the point?'

'Yes, quite terrible, quite absurd and even quite ridiculous, which is even worse,' continued the Count; 'if I were in London or Paris, perhaps I could laugh at it all with you, but here, in Naples...'

'You're going to keep a straight face; isn't that what you're trying to say?'

'Precisely.'

'Let's get down to the *fascino*,' said Miss Ward, impressed in spite of herself by Altavilla's gravity.

'This belief goes back to the very earliest times. It is alluded to in the Bible. Virgil speaks of it with conviction; the bronze amulets found in Pompeii, Herculaneum, and Stabia, the protective signs drawn on the walls of the houses that have been dug up, show how widespread this superstition once was.' (Altavilla maliciously emphasised the word *superstition*.) 'The entire Orient still believes in it, even these days. Red or green hands are painted on each side of a Moorish house to avert the evil influence. You can see a hand sculpted on the keystone of the Gate of Judgement in the Alhambra; all of which proves that this *prejudice* is at least very ancient even if it has no real foundation. When millions of men for thousands of years have shared a certain opinion, it is probable that this so generally accepted opinion was based on positive facts, on a long series of observations justified by the way events turned out... I find it difficult to believe, however high an opinion I have of myself, that

35

so many people, several of whom were certainly perfectly illustrious, enlightened and knowledgeable, could have been so crassly mistaken in a matter where I alone see things aright...'

'Your reasoning can easily be refuted,' interrupted Miss Alicia Ward, 'was not polytheism the religion of Hesiod, Homer, Aristotle, Plato, and even Socrates, who sacrificed a cock to Aesculapius, and a host of other persons of indubitable genius?'

'No doubt, but there is no longer anyone these days who sacrifices oxen to Jupiter.'

'It's better to use them for beefsteaks and rump steaks,' said the commodore sententiously, who had always been shocked by the habit of barbecuing the fat thighs of sacrificial beasts in Homer.

'No one offers doves to Venus, or peacocks to Juno, or goats to Bacchus; Christianity has replaced those dreams of white marble with which Greece peopled its Olympus; truth has made error evaporate, and yet numberless people still fear the effects of the *fascino* or, to give it its popular name, the *jettatura* or jinx.'

'That the ignorant populace at large should be worried by such influences I can well imagine,' said Miss Ward, 'but that a man of your high birth and your upbringing should share this belief is something I find quite astonishing.'

'More than one person who prides himself on being a freethinker,' replied the Count, 'hangs a horn on his window, nails antlers over his door, and won't take a single step unless he is draped with amulets; I'll be quite frank with you, for I have to confess without shame that when I meet a *jettatore*, I am only too keen to cross over to the other side of the street, and if I cannot avoid his gaze, I avert its effect as well as I can by making the time-honoured gesture. I make no more bones about it than a *lazzarone*, and I feel better that way. Numerous misadventures have taught me not to disdain these precautions.'

Miss Alicia Ward was a Protestant, brought up in great philosophical freedom of mind, who would accept nothing until she had examined it, and her rational nature found anything that could not be mathematically explained repugnant. The Count's speech surprised her. At first she inclined to think that he was simply joking; but Altavilla's calm and convinced tone of voice made her revise her ideas without however persuading her in the slightest.

'I grant you,' she said, 'that this prejudice exists, that it is widespread, that you are sincere in your fear of the evil eye, and aren't trying to make fun of the simplicity of a poor foreign girl; but give me some physical reason behind this superstitious idea, for, even if you were to judge me as a creature entirely devoid of poetry, I am highly sceptical: the fantastic, the mysterious, the occult, the inexplicable all have little hold over me.'

'You will not deny, Miss Alicia,' resumed the Count, 'the power of the human eye; the light of heaven combines in it with the reflection of the soul; the iris is a lens which concentrates the rays of life, and the spark of intellectual electricity springs from this narrow opening: doesn't the gaze of a woman pierce the hardest heart? Doesn't the gaze of a hero galvanise a whole army? Doesn't the gaze of the doctor tame the madman like a cold shower? Doesn't the gaze of a mother hold lions at bay?'

'You are pleading your case with eloquence,' replied Miss Ward, with a shake of her pretty head; 'forgive me if I still have my doubts.'

'And is the bird obeying a prejudice when, fluttering with horror and uttering lamentable shrieks, it comes down from a tree it could easily fly away from, to throw itself into the jaws of the snake that holds it fascinated? Has it heard, in its nest, feathery old gossips recounting stories of the *jettatura*? Haven't many effects been produced by causes that our organs are incapable of appreciating? Are the miasmas of malaria, plague, or cholera visible? No eye can make out the electric fluid on the spike of the lightning-rod, and yet the lightning is drawn off by it! What is absurd about supposing that a propitious or fateful beam can be emitted from a black, blue or grey iris? Why shouldn't that emanation bring fortune or misfortune in accordance with the mode of emission and the angle at which the object receives it?'

'It strikes me,' said the commodore, 'that the Count's theory has something specious about it; for my part, I've never been able to look into a toad's golden eyes without sensing an intolerable heat in my stomach, as if I had taken some emetic; and yet the poor reptile had more reason to be afraid than did I, who could crush him under my heel.'

'Ah! uncle! if you side with Mr d'Altavilla', said Miss Ward, 'I will be beaten. I don't have the strength for a fight. Although I might have many objections to raise against this ocular electricity which no physicist has ever mentioned, I am prepared to accept its existence for a moment; but how can the immense horns you so graciously presented to me possibly have any protective power against their ill effects?'

'Just as the lightning-rod draws off the lightning with its spike,' replied Altavilla, 'so the sharp tips of those horns on which the *jettatore*'s gaze is fixed drain away the harmful fluid and strip it of its dangerous electricity. Fingers crooked forward and coral amulets perform the same office.'

'What you're telling me is quite crazy, Count,' resumed Miss Ward, 'and this is what I think I have grasped: in your view, I am supposed to be under the influence of the *fascino* of a highly dangerous *jettatore*; and you have sent me horns to defend me against it?'

'I am afraid so, Miss Alicia,' said the Count, in the tones of the deepest conviction.

'I'd like to see one of those squint-eyes devils trying to fascinate my niece!' exclaimed the commodore. 'Although I am the wrong side of sixty, I haven't forgotten what I learnt in my boxing lessons yet.'

And he clenched his fist, his thumb pressing tight into his serried fingers.

'You only need two fingers, milord,' said Altavilla, taking the commodore's hand and putting it in the right position. 'Usually, the *jettatura* is involuntary; it happens without those who possess this fateful gift knowing anything about it, and it often happens indeed that when the *jettatori* become aware of their grim power, they deplore its effects more than anyone; so they should be avoided and not mistreated. And with horns, pointed fingers, or forked coral branches, you can neutralise or at least weaken their influence.'

'Upon my soul, it is most strange,' said the commodore, impressed in spite of himself by Altavilla's sang-froid.

'I didn't know I was so hemmed in and harried by *jettatori*,' said Miss Alicia, whose curiosity was wakening, although her scepticism was just as great as it had been. 'I hardly leave this terrace except in the evenings when I go for a ride in the calash along the Villa Reale with my uncle, and I've never noticed anything that could justify your supposition. On whom do your suspicions rest?'

'They are not suspicions, Miss Ward; my certainty is total,' replied the young Italian count.

'I beg you, reveal the name of this fateful being?' said Miss Ward, with a slight hint of mockery in her voice.

Altavilla was silent.

'It's a good idea to know who we need to beware of,' added the commodore.

The young Neapolitan count appeared to turn things over in his mind; then he stood up, stopped in front of Miss Ward's uncle, bowed respectfully to him and said to him:

'Milord Ward, I am asking for your niece's hand in marriage.'

At this unexpected phrase, Alicia flushed pink all over, and the commodore's face went from red to deep scarlet.

To be sure, Count Altavilla was a worthy suitor for Miss Ward's hand; he belonged to one of the most ancient and noble families in Naples; he was handsome, young, rich, held in great esteem, perfectly well bred, and irreproachable in his elegance; so his request, in itself, had nothing shocking about it; but it came in such a sudden, strange manner; it seemed to jar so greatly with the conversation they had started up, that the stupefaction of uncle and niece was by no means out of place. So Altavilla appeared neither surprised nor discouraged at it, and awaited the reply with steadfast poise.

'My dear Count,' the commodore finally said, once he had recovered his composure somewhat, 'your proposal astonishes me – just as much as it honours me. To tell you the truth, I don't know how to reply; I haven't consulted my niece. We were talking about *fascino*, *jettatura*, horns, amulets, open or closed hands, all sorts of things which have nothing to do with marriage, and then you suddenly ask for Alicia's hand! There's no logical link between them, and you will have to forgive me if I don't have any clear ideas on the subject. This union would certainly be perfectly proper, but I thought my niece had other intentions. It's true that an old sea dog like myself can't always read very well into the hearts of young women...'

Alicia, seeing her uncle becoming confused, took advantage of the silence he subsided into after his last sentence to bring to a close a scene that was becoming embarrassing, saying to the Neapolitan:

'Count, when a gallant man asks in all sincerity for the hand of an honest young woman, she has no call to be offended, but she does have the right to be astonished at the strange shape this request has assumed. I was begging you to tell me the name of the alleged *jettatore* whose influence may in your view be harmful to me, and you suddenly make my uncle a proposal the reason for which I cannot make out.'

'The reason,' said Altavilla, 'is that a gentleman does not gladly turn into an informer, and only a husband can defend his wife. But take a few days to think it over. Until then, the horns, if displayed where everyone can see them, will be sufficient, I hope, to guarantee your safety from any disagreeable event.'

That said, the Count rose and left with a deep bow.

Vicè, the tawny servant with frizzy hair, coming to take away the teapot and the cups, had, as she slowly came up the steps to the terrace, heard the end of the conversation; she nursed against Paul d'Aspremont all the aversion that a peasant woman of the Abruzzi, tamed by barely two or three years of domesticity, can feel towards a *forestiere* suspected of *jettatura*; in addition, she found Count Altavilla a splendid fellow, and could not imagine how Miss Ward could prefer to him a pale, puny young man that she, Vicè, could never have desired, even if he hadn't had the *fascino*. So, failing to appreciate the delicacy of the Count's procedure and desiring to take her mistress, whom she loved, out of the reach of a harmful influence, Vicè bent down towards Miss Ward's ear and said to her:

'*I* know the name that Count Altavilla is concealing from you.'

'I forbid you to tell it me, Vicè, if you want to stay in my good graces,' replied Alicia. 'Really, all these superstitions are shameful, and I will defy them as a good Christian girl who fears God alone.'

CHAPTER SEVEN

'*Jettatore! jettatore!* These words really were meant for me,' Paul d'Aspremont said to himself as he returned to his hotel; 'I don't know what they mean, but they must certainly have some insulting or mocking sense. What is so strange, unusual or ridiculous in my person to attract anyone's attention in such an unfavourable way? It seems to me, although no one is a good judge of himself, that I am neither handsome, nor ugly, nor tall, nor short, nor thin, nor fat, and that I can pass by unnoticed in a crowd. There is nothing eccentric about the way I dress; I'm not wearing a turban lit by candles like M. Jourdain in the ceremony of *Le Bourgeois gentilhomme*; I don't wear a jacket with a golden sun stitched on the back; there isn't a Negro walking ahead of me playing the timpani; my individual personality, which in any case is perfectly unknown in Naples, is hidden beneath the standard costume, the cloak of modern civilisation, and I am in every point identical with the elegant men about town who stroll along the Via Toledo or the Largo del Palazzo, albeit I perhaps have a slightly smaller cravat, a slightly less flashy tie-pin, a slightly less embroidered shirt, a slightly less showy waistcoat, a slightly smaller number of golden chains and a great deal fewer curls.

'Perhaps I don't have enough curls! Tomorrow I'll ask the hotel hairdresser to give me a going-over with the curling tongs. And yet people here are used to seeing foreigners, and a few barely noticeable differences in dress aren't enough to justify the mysterious word and the bizarre gesture that my presence provokes. Furthermore, I have noticed an expression of antipathy and fright in the eyes of people who move out of my way to avoid me. Whatever can I have done to those people, whom I am meeting for the first time? A traveller, a shadow passing by never to return, arouses nothing more than indifference wherever he goes, unless he is arriving from some distant region and is seen as the specimen of an unknown race: but every week the liners disgorge onto the pier thousands of tourists from whom I am not in the slightest bit different. Who bothers about it, except for the *facchini*, the hotel proprietors and the domestic staff of the place? I haven't killed my brother, since I never had one, and God cannot have inflicted the mark of Cain on me; and yet men seem troubled when they see me, and give me a wide berth: in Paris, in London, in Vienna, in all the cities where I have lived, I've never noticed that I produced any such effect; people have sometimes considered me haughty, disdainful, standoffish; I have been told that I affected an English sneer, that I imitated Lord Byron, but everywhere I have received the welcome due to a gentleman, and any advances I made, infrequent as they were, were all the better appreciated. A crossing of three days from Marseilles to Naples can't have changed me to the point where I have become odious or grotesque, I who have found favour with more than one woman and who have been capable of touching the heart of Miss Alicia Ward, a delightful young woman, a heavenly creature, an angel from Thomas Moore!'[21]

These reflections, reasonable enough to be sure, calmed Paul d'Aspremont to some extent, and he convinced himself that he had attributed to the exaggerated expressions of the Neapolitans, the people who gesticulate the most energetically in the whole world, a meaning of which they were innocent.

It was late. All the travellers, with the exception of Paul, had retired to their respective rooms; Gelsomina, the servant woman whose physiognomy we have already sketched in the discussion held in the kitchen under the presidency of Virgilio Falsacappa, waited for Paul to return before barring the entrance. Nanella, the other servant, whose turn it was to do the night duty, had begged her bolder colleague to take her place, not wishing to encounter the *forestiere* suspected of being able to put a jinx on people; and so Gelsomina was armed: an enormous bundle of amulets was bristling at her breast, and five little coral branches, instead of pendants of cut pearl, were dangling from her ears; her hand, clenched in advance, was extending its index and little fingers with a precision that the reverend father Andrea de Jorio, the author of the *Mimica degli antichi investigata nel gestire napoletano*, would assuredly have approved.[22]

Brave Gelsomina, concealing her hand in a fold of her skirt, presented the torch to M. d'Aspremont, and levelled at him a sharp, persistent, almost provocative gaze, of so strange an expression that the young man lowered his eyes: a circumstance which seemed to give considerable pleasure to this beautiful young woman.

Seeing her erect and motionless, holding out the torch with a statuesque gesture, her profile clearly standing out in the light, her eyes fixed and fiery, you would have thought she was the ancient figure of Nemesis seeking to disconcert a guilty man.

When the traveller had climbed the stairs and his footsteps had faded away in the silence, Gelsomina looked up triumphantly and said, 'I pushed his gaze back into his eyes I did, fair and square, that nasty man, may San Gennaro confound him; I'm sure nothing bad will happen to me.'

Paul slept badly and his sleep was restless; he was tormented by all sorts of bizarre dreams relating to the ideas that had preoccupied his waking hours: he saw himself surrounded by monstrous, grimacing figures, filled with expressions of hatred, anger, and fear; then these figures vanished; long, skinny, bony fingers, with gnarled joints, emerging from the shadow and illuminated by a red, hellish glow, threatened him with cabalistic signs; the nails of these fingers, curved into tigers' claws and vultures' talons, drew closer and closer to his face and seemed bent on gouging his eyes out of their sockets. Making a supreme effort, he managed to ward off these hands, which went fluttering up on bats' wings; but these crooked fingers were succeeded by the horns of oxen and buffalo, and the antlers of stags, whitened skeletons animated by a dead life, which assailed him with their horns and their antlers and forced him to throw himself into the sea, where he tore his body on a forest of coral with sharp or forked branches; a wave swept him up onto the shore, worn out, broken, half dead; and, like Lord Byron's Don Juan, he could just make out through his faintness a charming face bending over him; it wasn't Haydée[23], but Alicia, even more beautiful than the imaginary being created by the poet. The young woman was making vain efforts to drag up onto the sand the body that the sea was trying to claw back, and kept asking Vicè, the tawny servant, for help which the latter refused her, uttering a ferocious laugh: Alicia's arms were starting to tire, and Paul was pulled back into the depths.

These bewildering and alarming phantasmagorias, vague and horrifying, and others even more elusive still that recalled the shapeless ghosts just discernible in the opaque shadows of Goya's aquatints, tortured the sleeper until first light; his soul, freed from the numbness of his body, seemed to guess at what his waking thoughts could not understand, and tried to translate his presentiments into images in the dark chamber of his dream.

Paul got up broken and disquieted, as if he had been put on the trail of a hidden misfortune by these nightmares whose mystery he was afraid to sound; he turned in circles around the fateful secret, closing his eyes so as not to see and his ears so as not to hear; never had he felt more sad; he even doubted Alicia; the air of fatuous contentment worn by the Neapolitan count, the indulgence with which the young woman listened to him, the commodore's approving expression, all this flooded back to his memory embellished by a thousand cruel details, drowning his heart in bitterness and making his melancholy even more intense.

Light has this privilege, that it can disperse the malaise caused by nocturnal visions. Smarra[24], taking offence, flees with a flap of his membranous wings, when the day shoots its golden arrows into the bedroom through the gap between the curtains. The sun was shining merrily, the sky was clear, and on the sea's blue there sparkled millions of points of light; little by little Paul regained his tranquillity; he forgot his disturbing dreams and the strange impressions of the night before, or if he did think of them, it was to reproach himself with wild fancies.

He went out for a stroll to Chiaia to enjoy the spectacle of Neapolitan petulance: the merchants were crying their wares in a bizarre singsong in popular dialect, unintelligible to him, since he knew only Italian; they accompanied their words with chaotic gestures and a fury of action unknown in the north; but each time he stopped near a shop, the shopkeeper would look alarmed, murmur some imprecation in a low voice, and make a gesture with his fingers extended as if he would have liked to stab him with his little finger and his forefinger; the gossipy women, bolder than the shopkeepers, hurled insults at him and shook their fists.

CHAPTER EIGHT

M. d'Aspremont believed, on hearing himself insulted by the populace of Chiaia, that he was the object of those coarse and burlesque litanies with which fishmongers regale well-dressed people passing through the market-place; but such a strong sense of revulsion, such an authentic fright could be read in every eye that he was forced to abandon this interpretation; the word *jettatore*, which had already fallen on his ears in the San Carlino theatre, was uttered yet again, and with a threatening expression this time; so he slowly walked away, not fixing his gaze, the cause of such great disturbance, on anything. Keeping close to the houses so as to evade public attention, Paul reached the stall of a second-hand bookseller; he stopped, picked up and flicked through a few books, trying to keep an air of composure: in this way he turned his back on the passers-by, and as his face was half hidden by the book's pages he gave no opportunity for insult. The thought had indeed momentarily crossed his mind that he could lay into that riff-raff with his cane; but the vague superstitious terror that was starting to invade him had held him back. He remembered that once, when he had struck an insolent coachman with a light switch, he had caught him across the temple and killed him on the spot, an involuntary murder which he had never forgiven himself for. Having picked up and put back several volumes, he came across the treatise on *jettatura* by Signor Nicola Valetta[25]; this title dazzled his eyes as if written in letters of flame, and the book appeared placed there by the hand of destiny; he flung the six or eight *carlini*, the price of the book, to the bookseller who was looking at him mockingly while fiddling with two or three black horns intermingled with the charms on his watch; then he rushed back to his hotel, shut himself up in his room and started reading the book that would enlighten him and explain the suspicions that had obsessed him ever since the first days of his stay in Naples.

Signor Valetta's book is as easily available in Naples as are the *Secrets of Albert the Great*, the *Etteila* or the *Key to Dreams* in Paris. Valetta defines *jettatura*, and teaches the reader by what marks he can recognise it, and by what means protect himself from it; he divides *jettatori* into several classes, according to their degree of malevolence, and discusses all the questions that are raised by this grave subject.

If he had found this book in Paris, d'Aspremont would have leafed distractedly through it as if it were an old almanac stuffed full of ridiculous tales, and he would have laughed at the solemnity with which the author treats this nonsense; in the state of mind he found himself in, outside his natural environment, predisposed to credulity by a host of little incidents, he read it with a secret horror, like a layman spelling out in an arcane book of magic the words to summon up spirits and cabalistic formulae. Although he had not tried to pierce them, the secrets of hell revealed themselves to him; he could no longer prevent himself from knowing them, and now he was fully aware of his fateful power; he was a *jettatore*! He had to acknowledge the truth of the matter: he possessed all the distinctive signs described by Valetta.

It sometimes happens that a man who, up until now has believed himself to be gifted with perfect health, opens a medical book, either by chance or to pass the time, and on reading the pathological description of an illness, recognises that he is afflicted by it; enlightened by a fateful flash of insight, he feels at every symptom mentioned some obscure organ shuddering within him, or some hidden fibre of whose role in the body he had been unaware, and he pales as he realises that a death he thought was still a good way off is so imminent. Paul felt a similar effect.

He stood in front of a mirror and gazed at himself with frightening intensity: that composite perfection, the result of beauties that are not usually found together, made him resemble more than ever the fallen archangel, and gleamed with a sinister light in the dark depths of the mirror; the fibrils of his eyes twisted and turned like convulsive vipers; his eyebrows quivered like the bow from which the deadly arrow has just taken wing; the white furrow in his brow recalled the scar left by a bolt of lightning, and in his gleaming hair hellish flames seemed to be flickering; the marble pallor of his skin exacerbated each feature of this truly terrible physiognomy.

Paul felt frightened by himself – it seemed to him that the emanation of his eyes, reflected by the mirror, reverberated towards him in the shape of poisoned darts, like Medusa gazing at her horrible and charming head in the fawn reflection of a bronze shield.

The reader will perhaps object that it is difficult to believe that a young man of the world, imbued with modern science, having lived in the midst of all the scepticism of civilisation, could have taken seriously a popular prejudice, and imagined himself fatefully endowed with a mysterious and malevolent power. But we can only answer that there is an irresistible magnetism in the way people around you think, which affects you in spite of yourself, and against which the will-power of a single person is not always able to struggle to any effect: a man will arrive in Naples with nothing but mockery for the *jettatura*, only to finish by decking himself out with precautionary horn and fleeing in terror from any individual with a suspect eye. Paul d'Aspremont found himself in an even more serious situation: he himself had the *fascino*, and everyone was avoiding him, or else continually made the protective signs recommended by Signor Valetta in his presence. Although his reason revolted against such a conclusion, he could not stop himself recognising that he presented all the distinguishing marks that usually betray a *jettatore*.

The human mind, even the most enlightened, always keeps some dark corner where the hideous chimeras of credulity still lurk, and the bats of superstition hang from the ceiling. Ordinary life itself is so full of insoluble problems that the impossible becomes probable. You can believe or deny everything: from a certain point of view, dreams exist just as much as reality.

Paul felt himself overwhelmed by an immense sadness. He was a monster! Although endowed with the most affectionate instincts and the most benevolent nature, he brought misfortune in his wake; his gaze, involuntarily loaded with poison, harmed all those on whom it came to rest, even if his intentions were friendly. He possessed the dreadful privilege of gathering, concentrating, and distilling the morbid miasmas, dangerous electricity, and fateful influences of the atmosphere, and shooting them into the world around him. Several of the circumstances of his life which had seemed obscure to him hitherto and which he had blamed on chance were now bathed in a livid light: he remembered all sorts of enigmatic misadventures, unexplained misfortunes, catastrophes without a cause, which he could now explain; his mind drew bizarre conclusions and confirmed the low opinion he had formed of himself.

He went back over his life year by year: he remembered his mother who had died while giving birth to him, the unfortunate end of his little school friends, the dearest of whom had been killed in a fall from a tree which he, Paul, was watching him climb; that boating excursion which had begun so merrily with two friends, and from which he had returned alone, after unprecedented efforts to pull from the weeds the bodies of the poor boys drowned when the boat had capsized; the duel in which his foil, snapping off near the button and thus transformed into a rapier, had so dangerously wounded his opponent – a young man of whom he was very fond. Of course, it might all have a rational explanation, and Paul had always found one up to now; and yet, the accidental and chance nature of these events seemed to him to depend on another cause now that he knew Valetta's book: the fateful influence, the *fascino*, the *jettatura*, were undoubtedly responsible for their share of these catastrophes. Such a continuity of misfortunes around one and the same character was not *natural*.

Another, more recent circumstance came to his mind, in all its horrible details, and contributed considerably to strengthening him in his distressing belief.

In London, he often went to the Queen's Theatre, where the grace of a young English dancing-girl had particularly captivated him. Without being more enamoured of her than one can be of a gracious figure in a painting or an engraving, he followed her with his eyes among her companions in the corps de ballet, across the whirl of the choreographic manoeuvres; he loved that sweet, melancholy face, that delicate pallor which was never flushed by the animation of the dance, that lovely blond hair, lustrous and silky, crowned, depending on her role, with stars or flowers, those far-away eyes gazing out into space, those shoulders, chastely virginal as they quivered in his opera-glasses, those legs reluctant to kick up their cloudy gauze and shining in their silk like the marble of an ancient statue; each time she passed in front of the footlights, he greeted her with some small furtive sign of admiration, or armed himself with his pince-nez to get a better view of her.

One day, the dancer, swept along by the circular momentum of a waltz, grazed too closely that glittering line of flames which in the theatre separates the ideal world from the real world; her light sylph's draperies were fluttering like the wings of a dove about to take flight. A gas burner stuck out its blue and white tongue, and reached the aerial fabric. In an instant, flames enveloped the girl who danced for a few seconds more like a will-o'-the-wisp in the middle of a red flare of light, and then flung herself into the wings, panic-stricken, out of her mind with terror, consumed alive by her blazing clothes. Paul had been most painfully affected by this misfortune, which all the newspapers of the day mentioned – you could discover the victim's name in them, if you were curious to find out. But his sorrow was not mixed with any remorse. He attributed no part of the blame for the accident to himself, deploring it more than anyone.

Now he was convinced that his obstinacy in pursuing her with his gaze had not been unconnected with the death of that charming creature. He considered himself to be her assassin; he was horrified at himself and wished he had never been born.

This prostration was succeeded by a violent reaction; he broke out into a strained laugh, sent Valetta's book flying to the devil, and exclaimed, 'Honestly, I'm turning into an idiot or a madman! My head must have been exposed to the sun of Naples for too long. What would my friends in the club say if they learnt that I have seriously been mulling over this great question that weighs on my conscience – whether or not I am a *jettatore*!

Paddy knocked discreetly at the door. Paul opened it, and the groom, punctilious in his service, presented to him on the polished leather of his hat, while apologising for not having a silver tray, a letter from Miss Alicia.

M. d'Aspremont broke the seal and read the following words:

Are you avoiding me, Paul? You didn't come yesterday evening, and your lemon sorbet melted away in melancholy on the table. Until nine o'clock I kept my ears pricked, trying to make out the noise of the wheels of your carriage through the obstinate singing of the crickets and the thrum of tambourines; then I had to abandon all hope, and I quarrelled with the commodore. So much for woman's admirable sense of fairness! Are Pulcinella with his black nose, Don Limon and

Donna Pangrazia so full of charm for you? I know through my spies that you spent your evening at San Carlino. Of those allegedly important letters you did not write a single one. Why not confess quite openly, once and for all, that you are jealous of Count Altavilla? I thought you had more pride, and such modesty on your part touches me. Have no fear, Mr d'Altavilla is too handsome, and Apollos with lucky charms are not my type. I ought to display a sovereign indifference towards you and tell you that I didn't even notice your absence; but the truth is that I found the time very long, that I was in a very bad mood, feeling very irritable, and that I almost beat Vicè, who was laughing like a madwoman – and I don't even know why.

– A. W.

This playful, mocking letter quickly brought Paul's ideas back to real life. He dressed, ordered his carriage to be brought, and soon the Voltairean Scazziga was cracking his sceptical whip round the ears of his horses who set off at the gallop over the lava paving-stones, across the crowds that were still as dense as ever on the Santa Lucia quayside.

'Scazziga, whatever has got into you? You're going to cause an accident!' exclaimed M. d'Aspremont. The coachman immediately turned to reply, and Paul's angry eyes fell full on his face. A stone that Scazziga had not noticed made one of the front wheels bounce up, and the violence of the jolt made him fall off his seat, but without letting go of the reins. Agile as a monkey, he leapt back into his place, with a bump on his forehead as big as a hen's egg.

'The devil take me if I ever turn round again when you talk to me!' he muttered through his teeth. 'Timberio, Falsacappa and Gelsomina were right – he's a *jettatore*! Tomorrow, I'm going to buy a pair of horns. Even if it doesn't do any good, it can't do any harm.'

This brief incident made an unpleasant impression on Paul; it brought him back within the magic circle he was trying to escape from: every day a wheel runs over a stone, a clumsy coachman lets himself fall off his seat, there's nothing simpler and more commonplace. And yet the *effect* had followed the *cause* so closely – Scazziga's fall coincided so exactly with the *gaze* he had directed at him, that his apprehensions returned:

'I would really like,' he said to himself, 'to leave this crazy country tomorrow, where I feel my brain bouncing around in my skull like a dry hazelnut in its shell. But if I confide my fears to Miss Ward, she will laugh at them, and the climate of Naples is good for her health. Her health! But she was perfectly well before she knew me! Never had that swans' nest bobbing on the waves called England ever produced a child more pink and white! Life sparkled in her brilliant eyes, and blossomed on her fresh satin cheeks; a rich pure blood ran in blue veins beneath her transparent skin; you could sense through her beauty a gracious strength! See how she has grown pale under my gaze, thinner, quite changed! How her delicate hands have become frail! How those dancing eyes of hers are now surrounded by soft shadows! It is as if consumption has laid its bony fingers on her shoulder. In my absence, she quickly regained her bright colours; her breathing comes and goes easily in her chest, which the doctor had started to listen anxiously to; delivered from my harmful influence, she would live a good long life. Is it I who am killing her? The other evening didn't she feel, while I was there, a pain so acute that her cheeks lost their colour, as at the chill wind of death? Am I not casting a *jettatura* on her without wishing to? But perhaps there is a perfectly natural explanation for all this. Many young English women are predisposed to lung disease.'

These thoughts preoccupied Paul d'Aspremont throughout his journey. When he presented himself on the terrace, the place where Miss Ward and the commodore usually passed their time, the immense horns of the oxen of Sicily, Count Altavilla's present, were curving their crescents of jasper exactly where they could best be seen. Perceiving that Paul had noticed them, the commodore turned blue: this was his way of blushing, for, less delicate than his niece, he had been taken into Vicè's confidence…

Alicia, with a gesture of perfect disdain, motioned the servant woman to take the horns away, and fixed on Paul her lovely eyes filled with love, courage, and faith.

'Leave them in their place,' Paul told Vicè; 'they look really fine.'

Paul's observation about the horns given by Count Altavilla seemed to please the commodore; Vicè smiled, showing her teeth whose separate, pointed canines shone with a fierce whiteness; Alicia, with a rapid glance at her friend, seemed to be asking him a question that remained unanswered.

An embarrassed silence ensued.

The first minutes of even a cordial, familiar visit, one that is expected and renewed every day, are ordinarily rather strained. During the period of absence, even if it has lasted only a few hours, around each of the acquaintances has formed once more an invisible atmosphere against which all effusiveness is powerless. It is like a perfectly transparent window which lets you see the landscape but which a fly cannot cross. There is nothing there, apparently, and yet you can sense the obstacle.

At the back of the minds of the three members of this group, usually more at ease, lurked a thought which their wide experience of the world caused them to conceal. The commodore was twiddling his thumbs with a mechanical movement; d'Aspremont was gazing obstinately at the black polished tips of the horns which he had forbidden Vicè to take away, like a naturalist trying to classify, on the basis of a single fragment, an unknown species; Alicia was poking her finger into the bow of the wide ribbon pulled round her muslin dressing-gown, pretending to be tightening the knot.

It was Miss Ward who was the first to break the ice, with that playful freedom of young Englishwomen who become so modest and reserved with marriage.

'Really, Paul, you haven't been very nice recently. Perhaps your gallantry is a cold house-plant that can only blossom in England, and whose development is hindered by the high temperature of this climate? How attentive and zealous you were, always fussing around me in our Lincolnshire cottage! You would approach me with your lips puckered and your hand on your heart, your hair irreproachably curled, ready to sink to one knee in front of your soul's idol; in a word, looking just like the lovers depicted in the vignettes of novels.'

'I still love you, Alicia,' replied d'Aspremont in a deep voice, but without taking his eyes off the horns hanging from one of the ancient columns supporting the roof of vines.

'You say that in such a gloomy tone that I'd have to be a real coquette to believe it,' continued Miss Ward; 'I imagine that what you liked about me was my pale complexion, my diaphanous appearance, my Ossianic and misty grace; my state of suffering gave me a certain romantic charm that I've lost.'

'Alicia! You have never been more beautiful!'

'"Words, words, words," as Shakespeare has it. I am so beautiful that you won't even deign to look at me.'

And indeed, M. d'Aspremont's eyes had not turned even once towards the young woman.

'Come now,' she said, heaving a comically exaggerated sigh, 'I can see that I have become a big fat peasant girl, fresh-complexioned, high in colour, ruddy-cheeked, without the least elegance, incapable of appearing at the Almanach ball, or in a book of beauties, separated from an admiring sonnet by a leaf of tissue paper.'

'Miss Ward, you take pleasure in slandering yourself,' said Paul, with downcast eyes.

'You'd do better to admit frankly to me that I look dreadful. It's your fault too, commodore; with your chicken wings, your veal cutlets, your fillets of beef, your little glasses of Canary wine, your horse riding, your sea bathing, and your gymnastic exercises, you have managed to fashion a middle-class health for me, which dispels M. d'Aspremont's poetic illusions.'

'You are tormenting M. d'Aspremont and you are making fun of me,' said the commodore in response to this ribbing; 'but to be sure, fillet of beef is a substantial dish, and Canary wine has never done anyone any harm.'

'What a disappointment, my poor Paul! to leave a nixie, an elf, a wili, and to come back and find what doctors and relatives call a young woman of sound constitution! But listen to me, since you are no longer brave enough to look me in the eye, and are shuddering with horror. I weigh seven ounces more than when I left England.'

'Eight ounces!' the commodore interrupted with pride: he looked after Alicia the way the most devoted of mothers would have done.

'Is it exactly eight ounces? You terrible uncle, do you want to put M. d'Aspremont off me for good?' said Alicia, pouting in feigned discouragement.

While the young woman was provoking him by these flirtatious remarks – which she would not have permitted herself to make, even to her fiancé, without good reason – M. d'Aspremont, in prey to his obsession and not wishing to harm Miss Ward by turning his fateful eyes upon her, continued to direct his gaze at the talismanic horns or let them wander vaguely across the immense stretch of blue visible from the terrace.

He was wondering whether it wasn't his duty to flee from Alicia, even if this meant appearing to be a man without faith or honour, and going off to finish his life on some desert island where, at least, his *jettatura* would fade away for lack of any human gaze to absorb it.

'I can see,' said Alicia, prolonging her teasing, 'what is making you so sombre and so serious; the time of our wedding has been arranged for one month from now; and you are having second thoughts at the idea of becoming the husband of a poor country girl who no longer has the slightest elegance. I will release you from your promise: you can marry my friend Miss Sarah Templeton, who eats pickles and drinks vinegar to stay slim!'

This image made her laugh, with the silvery clear laughter of youth. The commodore and Paul freely shared her hilarity.

When the last spark of her somewhat strained outburst of gaiety had faded away, she went over to d'Aspremont, took him by the hand, led him to the piano set up in the corner of the terrace, and said to him as she opened a book of music on the stand:

'My dear, you're not being very chatty today and "when you can't be bothered to say it, you can always sing it"; so you can help perform this duettino, the accompaniment isn't difficult: it's barely a matter of striking more than a few chords.'

Paul sat on the stool, and Miss Alicia stood next to him so that she could follow the score of the song. The commodore threw back his head, stretched out his legs and assumed a pose of anticipatory beatitude, for he had pretensions to being a connoisseur, claiming that he adored music; but by the sixth bar he was already sleeping the sleep of the just, a sleep that he insisted, despite his niece's teasing, in calling ecstatic appreciation – although it sometimes happened that he started snoring, which is not really a symptom of ecstasy.

The duettino was a light and lively melody, in the style of Cimarosa, to words by Metastasio, and we could not describe it any more aptly than by comparing it to a butterfly repeatedly fluttering through a sunbeam.

Music has the power of chasing off evil spirits: after a few phrases, Paul was no longer thinking of fingers warding off the evil eye, of magical horns, or of coral amulets; he had forgotten all about Signor Valetta's terrible book and all the bad dreams inspired in him by the *jettatura*. His soul was rising joyously up, with Alicia's voice, into the pure bright air.

The cicadas stayed silent as if to listen, and the sea breeze which had just risen was carrying away the notes along with the petals that had fallen from the flowers in the vases on the terrace ledge.

'My uncle sleeps like the Seven Sleepers in their cave. If he wasn't always dozing off like this, we might well take it as a slight to our musical skills,' said Alicia, closing the music book. 'While he's resting, would you like to come for a walk round the garden with me, Paul? I still haven't shown you my paradise.'

And she took from a nail stuck into one of the columns, where it was hanging by its ribbons, a broad-brimmed Florentine straw hat.

When it came to horticulture, Alicia professed the strangest principles; she thought one shouldn't pick flowers or trim branches; and what had charmed her about the villa was, as we have said, the wild, uncultivated state of the garden.

The young couple picked their way between clumps of vegetation which closed immediately behind them. Alicia walked in front and laughed to see Paul stung by the branches of the laurel roses that she brushed aside and that swung back to strike him. She had hardly gone a score of paces before the twigs of a branch, like a hand of greenery reaching out to play a trick on her, seized and held her straw hat, lifting it so high that Paul couldn't reach it.

Fortunately, the foliage was dense, and the sun barely cast a few golden sequins onto the sand through the gaps between the branches.

'This is my favourite retreat,' said Alicia, pointing out to Paul a fragment of rock with picturesque fissures, protected by a tangle of orange bushes, citrons, mastic trees and myrtles.

She sat down in a crevice shaped like a seat, and motioned to Paul to kneel before her on the thick dry moss that formed a carpet around the feet of the rock.

'Place both your hands in mine and look me full in the face. In a month's time, I will be your wife. Why are your eyes avoiding mine?'

For indeed, Paul, relapsing into his obsession with the *jettatura*, was averting his gaze.

'Are you frightened of reading in my eyes a hostile or guilty thought? You know my soul has been yours ever since the day you brought my uncle the letter of recommendation in the parlour at Richmond. I am from the race of those tender Englishwomen, romantic and proud, who in a single instant fall in love for their entire lives – for more than their lives, perhaps – and who know how to love and how to die. Immerse your gaze in mine, I want you to; don't try to lower your eyelids, don't turn away, or I'll start thinking that a gentleman who should fear God alone is allowing himself to be frightened by base superstitions. Fix on me that eye that you think is so terrible and that to me is so sweet, since I can see your love in it, and decide whether you find me pretty enough still to take me, when we are married, for a ride through Hyde Park in an open calash.'

Paul, filled with boundless love, fixed on Alicia a long gaze of passionate commitment. Suddenly the young woman turned pale; a shooting pain pierced her heart like the tip of an arrow: it seemed as if some fibre snapped in her chest, and she hastily put her handkerchief to her lips. A red spot stained the fine cambric, which Alicia quickly folded.

'Oh! thank you, Paul; you have made me really happy. I thought you didn't love me any more!'

Alicia's attempt to conceal her handkerchief hadn't been quite fast enough to prevent M. d'Aspremont from noticing it; a dreadful pallor spread over Paul's features, for an indisputable proof of his fateful power had just been given him, and the most sinister ideas went through his head; even the thought of suicide presented itself to him; wasn't it his duty to rid the world of himself, as a maleficent being, and thus annihilate the involuntary cause of so many unhappy events? He would have accepted on his own account the harshest trials and courageously borne life's burden; but to kill what he loved best in the whole world was surely far too horrible.

The heroic young woman had fought down the sensation of pain that followed Paul's gazing at her, and that confirmed so strangely the opinions of Count Altavilla. A mind less firm might have been struck by this consequence which was, if not supernatural, at least difficult to explain; but, as we have said, Alicia's soul was religious and not superstitious. Her unshakeable faith in what it is necessary to believe rejected as nursery stories all those tales of mysterious influences, and laughed at the most deeply rooted popular prejudices. Furthermore, even if she had admitted the *jettatura* as real, even if she had recognised the evident signs of its existence in Paul, her proud and tender heart would not have hesitated for a second. Paul had committed no action in which the most delicate and sensitive person would have found the slightest cause for criticism, and Miss Ward would have preferred to drop dead before that gaze, allegedly so harmful, rather than back out of a love accepted by her with her uncle's consent and soon to be crowned by marriage. Miss Alicia Ward somewhat resembled those heroines of Shakespeare, chastely bold, virginally resolute, whose capacity to fall suddenly in love does not make them any the less pure and faithful, and whom a single moment can bind to their beloved forever; her hand had pressed Paul's, and no other man in the world would ever hold it in his. She considered her life to be no longer free, and her sense of propriety would have rebelled at the mere idea of joining herself in wedlock to any other man.

So she showed a real gaiety, or one so well mimicked as to have deceived the most subtle observer, and raising Paul, still kneeling before her, to his feet, she led him through the flower- and plant-strewn paths of her overgrown garden, to a place where the vegetation left a gap through which you could make out the sea like a blue dream of infinity. This bright and serene prospect dispelled Paul's dark thoughts: Alicia was leaning on the young man's arm with confiding self-abandonment, as if she was already his wife. Through this pure, mute caress – insignificant if it had come from any other woman but decisive coming from her – she was giving herself to him even more deliberately, reassuring him against his terrors, and getting him to understand how little she was bothered by the dangers that were said to threaten her. Although she had imposed silence first on Vicè, then on her uncle, and although Count Altavilla hadn't named any specific name, though recommending her to protect herself from an evil influence, she had soon realised that it was Paul d'Aspremont he had in mind; the handsome Neapolitan's obscure references could allude only to the young Frenchman. She had also seen that Paul, yielding to the prejudice so widespread in Naples, which makes a *jettatore* of any man with a somewhat unusual physiognomy, believed himself affected by the *fascino*, thereby showing an inconceivable lack of psychological robustness, and was averting from her his eyes full of love, for fear of harming her with his gaze; so as to fight against this nascent obsession, she had instigated the whole scene we have just described, and which produced the opposite result from the one she had intended, since it anchored Paul more than ever in his fateful monomania.

The two lovers returned to the terrace, where the commodore, still under the sway of the music, was continuing to sleep melodiously on his bamboo easy chair. Paul took his leave, and Miss Ward, parodying the Neapolitan gesture of farewell, blew him from her fingertips an imperceptible kiss, saying, 'See you tomorrow, Paul?' in a voice laden with smooth caresses.

Alicia at this moment was radiantly, alarmingly, almost supernaturally beautiful: so much so that her uncle, woken with a start by the sound of Paul's exit, was struck by her appearance. The whites of her eyes assumed the tones of burnished silver and made her pupils sparkle like stars with luminous blackness; her cheek-bones were imbued with a hint of ideal pink, heavenly in its purity and ardour, a colour no painter ever managed to obtain on his palette; her temples, as transparent as agate, were filigreed by a skein of slender blue veins, and her whole flesh seemed shot through by rays of light: it was as if her soul was flooding out through her skin.

'How lovely you are today, Alicia!' said the commodore.

'You're spoiling me, uncle; and if I'm not the vainest little girl in all three kingdoms, it's no thanks to you. Luckily I don't believe in flattery, even when it's disinterested.'

'Lovely, dangerously lovely,' continued the commodore to himself; 'she reminds me, in every feature, of her mother, poor Nancy, who died at the age of nineteen. Angels like her cannot remain on earth: it seems that a breeze lifts them from the ground and invisible wings start to unfurl from their shoulders; they're too white, too pink, too pure, too perfect; their ethereal bodies lack the coarse red blood of life. God, who loans them to the world for a few days, is in a hurry to get them back. Her supreme radiance makes me as sad as if it were a farewell.'

'So, uncle, if I'm all that pretty,' resumed Miss Ward, seeing the commodore's brow darken, 'it's time for me to marry: the veil and the bridal crown will suit me.'

'Marry? Are you in such a hurry to leave your old redskin of an uncle, Alicia?'

'But I won't be leaving you; isn't it agreed with M. d'Aspremont that we'll be living together? You well know that I can't live without you.'

'M. d'Aspremont! M. d'Aspremont!... The wedding has yet to take place.'

'Doesn't he have your word... and mine? Sir Joshua Ward has never broken his word.'

'He has my word, there's no disputing it,' replied the commodore in evident embarrassment.

'Didn't the period of six months that you had fixed elapse... several days ago?' said Alicia, whose modest cheeks were growing even pinker, for this conversation, necessary given the point matters had now reached, put a strain on her delicate, sensitive disposition.

'Ah, you've been counting the months, my girl; one can never trust that discreet face!'

'I love M. d'Aspremont,' the young woman replied gravely.

'Ay, there's the rub,' said Sir Joshua Ward who, imbued as he was with the ideas of Vicè and Altavilla, was not desperately keen to have a *jettatore* as a son-in-law. 'If only you loved someone else!'

'I don't have two hearts,' said Alicia; 'I will have only one love, even were I, like my mother, to die at nineteen.'

'Die? Don't say such horrid words, I beg you,' exclaimed the commodore.

'Do you have anything to reproach M. d'Aspremont with?'

'Nothing, to be sure.'

'Has he failed in his honour in any way at all? Has he shown himself even once to be cowardly, base, lying or perfidious? Has he ever insulted a woman or retreated before a man? Is his coat of arms sullied by any secret stain? Would a young woman, taking his arm to go out into society, need to blush or lower her eyes?'

'M. d'Aspremont is a perfect gentleman, there is nothing to be said against his respectability.'

'Believe me, uncle: if any such reason existed, I would give up M. d'Aspremont this very hour, and bury myself in some inaccessible retreat; but no other reason, do you hear me, no other will make me break a sacred promise,' said Miss Alicia Ward in firm, gentle tones.

The commodore was twiddling his thumbs, a habit he resorted to when he didn't know what to say, to give himself an air of composure.

'Why have you started treating Paul so coldly?' continued Miss Ward. 'You used to be so fond of him; you couldn't do without him in our Lincolnshire cottage, and you used to say, as you shook his hand so powerfully you almost pulled his fingers off, that he was a praiseworthy young man, to whom you would be pleased to entrust a young woman's happiness.'

'Indeed, I was really fond of young Paul,' said the commodore, moved by those memories that his niece had evoked at just the right time; 'but what is shrouded in the fogs of England becomes clear in the sunlight of Naples…'

'What do you mean?' asked Alicia tremulously, her face suddenly washed of its bright colours and turning as white as an alabaster statue on a tomb.

'Well, your Paul is a *jettatore.*'

'What? *You*, uncle? You, Sir Joshua Ward, a gentleman, a Christian, a subject of Her Majesty the Queen, a former officer in the English fleet, an enlightened and civilised being, who can be consulted on any topic; you who are educated and wise, who read the Bible and the Gospels every evening, you don't hesitate to call Paul a *jettatore*! Oh, I really didn't expect that from you!'

'My dear Alicia,' replied the commodore, 'I am everything you've just said when you don't come into the picture, but when a danger, even an imaginary one, threatens you, I become more superstitious than a peasant from the Abruzzi, a *lazzarone* on the pier, an *ostricaio*[26] from Chiaia, a servant from Terra di Lavoro, or even a Neapolitan count. Paul can stare me in the face as much as he likes with his eyes whose rays of vision cross, and I'll remain as calm as if I stood before the tip of a sword or the barrel of a pistol. The *fascino* won't gain any purchase on my tanned hide, roughened and reddened by all the suns in the world. I only believe in it for your sake, dear niece, and I admit that I feel a cold sweat breaking out at my temples when the eyes of that unhappy boy rest on you. He has no evil intentions, I know, and he loves you more than his own life; but it seems to me that, under his influence, your features become drained, your colour disappears, and you try to conceal a sharp pain; and then I have a furious desire to poke out your M. Paul d'Aspremont's eyes with the tip of the horns given by Altavilla.'

'Poor, dear uncle,' said Alicia, touched by the commander's heated outburst; 'our lives are in God's hands; no prince dies on his parade bed, nor any sparrow beneath his tiled roofs, unless his time has been appointed on high; the *fascino* has nothing to do with it, and it's a mark of impiety to think that a gaze aimed more or less directly can have any influence. Let's see, nuncle,' she continued, using that affectionate term deployed by the Fool in *King Lear*, 'you weren't serious when you were talking just now; your affection for me was interfering with your judgement which is usually so astute. Come now, you wouldn't really dare to tell M. Paul d'Aspremont that you are withdrawing your niece's hand in marriage from him, the same hand you put in his, and that you don't want him as a son-in-law any more, on the fine pretext that he's a – *jettatore*!'

'By Joshua, my patron saint, who halted the sun!' exclaimed the commodore, 'I won't mince my words to that handsome M. Paul. I don't care a fig if I appear ridiculous, absurd, even unfair, when it's your health, and perhaps even your life, that's at stake! I had come to an agreement with a man, not a magician. I made a promise; well, I'm wriggling out of my promise, that's all; if he's not happy about it, I'll give him satisfaction.'

And the commodore, exasperated, made an imaginary lunge, without paying the least attention to the gout that was gnawing his toes.

'Sir Joshua Ward, you will do no such thing,' said Alicia, with calm dignity.

The commodore sank, out of breath, into his bamboo easy chair, and remained silent.

'Well, uncle, even if this odious and stupid accusation were true, should we for all that turn M. d'Aspremont away and convert his misfortune into a crime? Haven't you acknowledged that the evil he might bring about didn't depend on his will, and that there was never a soul more loving, more generous and more noble?'

'You don't marry vampires, however well-intentioned they might be,' replied the commodore.

'But all that's an illusion, a crazy superstition; what is true, unfortunately, is that Paul has been afflicted by these follies, which he has started to take seriously; he's scared, he's suffering from hallucinations; he believes he has this fateful power, he's afraid of himself, and every little accident he didn't even notice before, and which today he imagines he is the cause of, confirms this conviction in him. Isn't it up to me, I who am his wife in the sight of God, and who will soon be so in the sight of men – with your blessing, my dear uncle – to calm that overexcited imagination, to chase away those vain phantoms, to reassure, by my apparent and real safety, that haggard anxiety, closely akin to monomania, and so save, through happiness, that beautiful but troubled soul, that charming but imperilled mind?'

'You are always right, Miss Ward,' said the commodore; 'and although you call me wise, I'm just an old fool. I think that Vicè is a witch; she had turned my head with all her stories. As for Count Altavilla, his horns and his cabalistic knick-knacks seem to me pretty ridiculous right now. Doubtless, it was all a strategy he dreamt up so he could see off Paul and marry you himself.'

'Maybe Count Altavilla is acting in good faith,' said Miss Ward, with a smile; 'just now you still shared his opinion about the *jettatura*.'

'Don't abuse your advantages, Miss Alicia; anyway, I'm not so free of my error that I don't risk relapsing into it. The best thing would be to leave Naples by the first steamer, and return in peace and quiet to England. When Paul no longer sees ox horns, deer antlers, pointing fingers, coral amulets and all those diabolical devices, his imagination will calm down, and I too will forget all that nonsense that has almost made me break my word and commit an action unworthy of a gallant gentleman. You will marry Paul, since that's what we have agreed. You'll keep for me the parlour and the ground-floor bedroom in the house in Richmond, and the octagonal tower in the little Lincolnshire castle, and we'll all live happily together. If your health requires a warmer climate, we'll rent a country cottage near Tours, or else in Cannes, where Lord Brougham has a fine property, and where these damnable superstitions about the *jettatura* are unknown, thank God. What do you say to my plan, Alicia?'

'You don't need my approval, am I not the most obedient of nieces?'

'Yes, when I do what you want, you cunning little vixen,' said the commodore with a smile, as he stood up to go back to his room.

Alicia remained a few minutes longer on the terrace; but, either because this scene had led to her becoming overexcited and feverish, or because Paul really did exert on the young woman the influence feared by the commodore, the warm breeze, blowing across her shoulders protected by a simple gauze shawl, felt icy cold to her, and that evening, feeling unwell, she asked Vicè to spread over her cold marble-white feet one of those harlequin-patterned blankets made in Venice.

Meanwhile the fireflies were flickering across the lawn, the crickets were singing, and the round yellow moon was rising in the sky in a haze of heat.

CHAPTER ELEVEN

The next day, Alicia, who had not had a good night, barely sipped at the drink that Vicè prepared for her every morning, and languidly set it back down on the pedestal table next to her bed. She was not exactly in any pain, but she felt broken; it was more of a vague psychological malaise than a real illness, and she would have been hard pressed to describe the symptoms to a doctor. She asked Vicè for a mirror: a young woman is more worried about the way her beauty might be adversely affected by suffering than by the suffering itself. She was extremely pale; but two small flushes like two petals of a Bengal rose fallen into a saucer of milk were floating over the pallor. Her eyes were gleaming with an unusual brightness, lit by the fever's last flames; but the cherry colour of her lips was much less vivid, and to get some colour back into them, she gnawed them with her little pearly teeth.

She got up, wrapped herself in a white cashmere dressing-gown, wound a gauze scarf round her head – for, in spite of the heat which had set the cicadas singing, she was still feeling the cold slightly – and went out onto the terrace at the usual hour, so as not to awaken the ever-vigilant solicitude of the commodore. She picked at her breakfast, though not feeling at all hungry, as she knew that the slightest hint she felt unwell would without fail have been attributed to Paul's influence by Sir Joshua Ward, and this is what Alicia wanted above all else to avoid.

Then, on the pretext that the dazzling sunlight was tiring her, she withdrew to her room, not before she had reiterated several times to the commodore, whose suspicions tended to be aroused by such behaviour, her assurances that she was in splendid good health.

'Splendid... I doubt it,' said the commodore to himself when his niece had left. 'She had a pearly sheen round her eyes, and a high colour over her cheek-bones, just like her poor mother who also claimed that she had never been in better health. What should I do? To take Paul from her would simply mean killing her by other means; let's leave nature to follow its course. Alicia is so young! Yes, but it's the youngest and most beautiful that old Mab has her eye on; she's as jealous as a woman. What if I got a doctor to come? But what can a doctor do for an angel! And yet all the disturbing symptoms had disappeared... Ah! if it really were you, damned Paul, whose ill wind made that divine flower droop, I would strangle you with my own hands. Nancy didn't have any *jettatore* casting his evil eye on her, and yet she died. If Alicia were to die!... No, it's not possible. I've done nothing against God for him to reserve that dreadful sorrow for me. When she does die, I will have been sleeping for a good long while under my tombstone with its *Sacred to the Memory of Sir Joshua Ward*, in the shade of the church tower of my native soil. It will be she who comes to weep and pray over the grey stone for the old commodore... I don't know what's wrong with me, but I'm all melancholy, and devilish gloomy this morning!'

To dispel these black thoughts, the commodore added a little Jamaica rum to the tea that had gone cold in his cup, and had his hookah brought to him, an innocent distraction that he allowed himself only in Alicia's absence, as her delicate health might have been affected even by that light and fragrant smoke.

He had already boiled the aromatic water of the container and blown out a few bluish clouds of smoke, when Vicè appeared announcing Count Altavilla.

'Sir Joshua,' said the Count, after the first exchange of civilities, 'have you been thinking over the request I made to you the other day?'

'I have been thinking it over, yes,' replied the commodore, 'but, you know, M. Paul d'Aspremont has my word.'

'Doubtless; and yet there are cases where one's word can be taken back; for instance when the man to whom you have given it, for one reason or another, isn't the man you at first took him for.'

'Count, speak more clearly.'

'I hate having to accuse a rival; but, after the conversation we had together, you must understand me. If you were to reject M. Paul d'Aspremont, would you accept me as a son-in-law?'

'For my part, certainly; but it's not as sure that Miss Ward would go along with this substitution. Her head has been turned by this Paul, and it's to some extent my fault, for I myself gave the boy my favour before all these stupid stories started to go the rounds. Excuse the epithet, Count, but my brain really is topsy-turvy.'

'Do you want your niece to die?' said Altavilla emphatically and gravely.

'By Jove! my niece die?' exclaimed the commodore, bounding from his armchair and throwing down the morocco pipe of his hookah.

When this particular string was plucked in Sir Joshua Ward, it always reverberated loud and long.

'So is my niece dangerously ill?'

'Don't get alarmed so quickly, milord; Miss Alicia may live, and indeed perhaps for a good long time.'

'Thank goodness! you had given me a real panic.'

'But on one condition,' continued Count Altavilla, 'She must stop seeing M. Paul d'Aspremont.'

'Ah! I spy the *jettatura* hailing into view again! Unfortunately, Miss Ward doesn't believe in it.'

'Hear me out,' said Count Altavilla with composure. 'When I first met Miss Alicia at the ball at the Prince of Syracuse's, and conceived for her a passion as respectful as it was ardent, it was the radiant health, the joy of existence, the bloom of life that glowed in her whole person that struck me first. Her beauty was made bright by it, seeming to float in an atmosphere of well-being. This phosphorence made her shine like a star; she eclipsed the women of England, Russia, Italy, and I had eyes for her alone. To her British air of distinction she added the pure and strong grace of the ancient goddesses; excuse this mythological allusion in the descendant of a Greek colony.'

'It's true that she looked superb! Miss Edwina O'Herty, Lady Eleanor Lilly, Mrs Jane Strangford, and Princess Vera Fedorovna Baryatinsky were almost yellow with envy,' said the commodore in delight.

'And now can't you see that her beauty has started to take on a languishing air, that her features are starting to look less firm, more fragile and unhealthy, that the veins of her hands are standing out in darker blue than they should, that her voice sounds like a harmonica that produces a worrying vibrato and a painful charm? The earthly element is retreating and giving way to the angelic element. Miss Alicia is gaining an ethereal perfection that, even if this makes you think me materialistic, I don't like to see in the young women of this world.'

The Count's words echoed so closely the secret preoccupations of Sir Joshua Ward that he remained silent for a few minutes, as if lost in a profound reverie.

'All that is true; although I sometimes try to disguise the facts from myself, I can't deny what you say.'

'I haven't finished,' said the Count. 'Had Miss Alicia's health before the arrival of M. Paul d'Aspremont in England ever given any cause for concern?'

'Never: she was the freshest and merriest child in the three kingdoms.'

'M. d'Aspremont's presence coincides, as you can see, with the periods of ill-health that are undermining Miss Ward's precious constitution. I am not asking you, a man of the north, to give your implicit credence to a belief, a prejudice, a superstition, if you like, of our southern countries, but you must nonetheless agree that these facts are strange and deserve your full attention...'

'Couldn't Alicia just be ill... for natural reasons?' said the commodore, shaken by Altavilla's specious reasonings, but held back by a sort of English compunction from adopting the popular Neapolitan belief.

'Miss Ward isn't ill; she is falling victim to a sort of poisoned gaze, and if M. d'Aspremont is not a *jettatore*, he is at least a harmful presence.'

'What can I do about it? She loves Paul, laughs off the idea of a *jettatura* and claims you can't give a man of honour a reason like that for turning him down.'

'I have no right to take your niece under my wing: I am neither her brother, nor her parent, nor her fiancé; but if I could obtain your promise, perhaps I could make an effort to wrest her away from that fateful influence. Oh! you have nothing to fear; I will not do anything unwise; although I am young, I know that it is not done to cause a stir about a young woman's reputation; – but allow me to keep my plan quiet. Have enough faith in my honesty to believe that I have no intentions that would offend against even the most stringent sense of honour.'

'So you really do love my niece?' said the commodore.

'Yes, since I love her without hope; but will you grant me freedom of action?'

'You are a terrible man, Count Altavilla; well, all right! try to save Alicia your way, I won't have any objections and I may even approve.'

The Count stood up, bowed, returned to his carriage and told the coachman to drive him to the hotel Roma.

Paul, his elbows on the table, and his head in his hands, was immersed in the most painful thoughts; he had seen the two or three red droplets on Alicia's handkerchief, and, still infatuated with his jinx, he was reproaching himself for his murderous love; he thought he had been wrong to accept the devotion of this beautiful young woman who was prepared to die for him, and he wondered with what superhuman sacrifice he could repay that sublime self-abnegation.

Paddy, the gnome-like jockey, interrupted this meditation when he brought in Count Altavilla's visiting-card.

'Count Altavilla! what can he want with me?' said Paul, with considerable astonishment. 'Show him in.'

When the Neapolitan appeared on the threshold of his door, M. d'Aspremont had already hidden his surprise beneath that mask of glacial indifference which people in society use to conceal their reactions.

With a frigid politeness he motioned the Count to an armchair, sat down himself, and waited in silence, his eyes fixed on his visitor.

'Sir,' began the Count, fiddling with the lucky charms on his watch, 'what I have to say to you is so strange, so out of place, so improper, that you would be within your rights to throw me out of the window. Spare me that brutality, for I am ready to give you satisfaction as a gentleman.'

'I am listening, sir, but I may well later accept the offer you have just made, if what you have to say is not to my liking,' replied Paul, not a muscle in his face moving.

'You are a *jettatore*!'

At these words, a pallid green hue suddenly spread over M. d'Aspremont's face, red rings encircled his eyes; his eyebrows contracted, the crease in his forehead deepened, and from his eyes seemed to flash sulphurous sparks; he half rose, clawing with his clenched fingers the mahogany arms of his chair. He was so terrible in appearance that Altavilla, brave as he was, gripped one of the little forking branches of coral hanging from his watch-chain, and instinctively aimed its tips towards his interlocutor.

Making a supreme effort of will, M. d'Aspremont sat down again and said, 'You were right, sir; the recompense you suggested was indeed what an insult like that would deserve; but I will be patient enough to wait for another form of reparation.'

'Believe me when I tell you,' continued the Count, 'that I have not uttered this affront, which can be washed away only by bloodshed, to a gentleman without the most serious reasons. I love Miss Alicia Ward.'

'Why should that bother me?'

'Indeed, there is little enough reason for you to be bothered, since you are loved; but I, Don Felipe Altavilla, I forbid you to see Miss Alicia Ward.'

'I have no reason to take orders from you.'

'I know,' replied the Neapolitan count; 'and so I have no great hope that you will obey me.'

'So what is the reason that is impelling you to act?' said Paul.

'I am firmly convinced that the *fascino* with which you are unhappily endowed is having a fatal influence on Miss Alicia Ward. It's an absurd idea, a prejudice worthy of the Middle Ages, which must strike you as utterly ridiculous; I'm not going to argue with you on that score. Your eyes are drawn to Miss Ward and fixing on her, in spite of yourself, that pernicious gaze that will result in her death. I have no other way of preventing that unfortunate result than by seeking with you a spurious quarrel. In the sixteenth century I would have had you killed by one of my mountain peasants; but these days such customs are no longer appropriate. I did think of requesting you to return to France; it was too naive of me: you would have laughed at this rival telling you to go away and leave him alone with your fiancée under the pretext of a *jettatura*.'

While Count Altavilla was speaking, Paul d'Aspremont felt himself flooded by a secret horror; so he, a Christian, was prey to the powers of hell, and the angel of evil was looking out through his own eyes! He was sowing catastrophes, his love could kill! For an instant his reason spun in his brain, and madness beat with its wings against the inner walls of his skull.

'Count, on your honour, do you really believe what you are saying?' exclaimed d'Aspremont after several minutes of a reverie that the Neapolitan respected.

'On my honour, I do believe it.'

'Ah! so it must be true!' said Paul half aloud. 'So I am a murderer, a demon, a vampire! I am killing that heavenly creature, I am going to bring despair on that old man!' And he was on the point of promising the Count that he would never see Alicia again; but self-respect and jealousy which were stirring in his heart kept the words from leaving his lips.

'Count, I won't hide from you the fact that I am right now on my way to see Miss Ward.'

'I won't grab you by the collar to prevent you; you spared me any assault just now, I am grateful to you for that; but I will be delighted to see you, at six in the morning, in the ruins of Pompeii, in the *thermae*[27], for instance; it's the perfect spot. What is your weapon of choice? You are the injured party: sword, sabre, or pistol?'

'We will fight with knives, and blindfolded, separated by a handkerchief which we will each hold by one end. We must ensure we have an equal chance: I am a *jettatore*; I would merely have to fix my gaze on you to kill you, Signor Count!'

Paul d'Aspremont burst out into a strident laugh, pushed open a door and disappeared.

CHAPTER TWELVE

Alicia had settled into a room on the ground floor of the house, whose walls were decorated with those frescoed landscapes that, in Italy, replace wallpaper. The floor was covered with mats of Manila hemp. A table over which was draped a length of Turkish rug and strewn with books of poetry by Coleridge, Shelley, Tennyson, and Longfellow, a mirror with an antique frame, and a few rattan chairs comprised all the furnishing. The blinds hanging at the window and made from Chinese rush adorned with images of pagodas, rocks, willows, cranes, and dragons, were half open, filtering a gentle light into the room. The branch of an orange tree, loaded with flowers that the fruits, as they took shape, scattered to the ground, pushed through the open window and spread its branches like a garland above Alicia's head, sprinkling its snowy fragrance over her.

The young woman, still not feeling well, was lying on a narrow sofa near the window; two or three Morocco cushions raised her to a half-sitting position; the Venetian blanket was chastely wrapped round her feet; thus disposed, she could receive Paul without infringing the laws of English modesty.

The book Alicia had been reading had slipped from her distracted hand to the ground; her eyes were somewhat moist and unfocused under their long lashes, seemingly gazing beyond the world; she was filled with that almost voluptuous lassitude that follows an attack of fever, and her sole occupation was chewing at the flowers of orange blossom that she picked from her blanket and whose bitter fragrance she liked. Isn't there a picture of Venus munching on roses, by Schiavone?[28] What a gracious counterpart to the old Venetian's picture a modern artist would have been able to paint, if he had depicted Alicia nibbling orange flowers!

She was thinking of M. d'Aspremont and wondering if she really would live long enough to be his wife; not that she gave any credence to the influence of the jinx, but she felt herself overwhelmed against her will by funereal premonitions: that very night she had had a dream which had left her with an impression which had not been dispelled when she woke.

In her dream, she had been lying down but awake, and fixing her gaze on the door of her room, sensing that *someone* was about to appear. After two or three minutes of anxious expectation, she had seen, detaching itself from the dark background framed by the door, a slender white shape which, at first transparent and, like a light mist, allowing you to see objects through it, had taken on greater consistency as it advanced towards the bed.

The shade was dressed in a muslin dress which fell in folds to the ground; long coils of black hair, half unwound, were cascading mournfully down her pale face, marked with two little pink spots on her cheek-bones; the flesh of her neck and breast was so white that it merged with her dress, and you couldn't have said where the skin ended and the fabric began; an almost imperceptible Venetian chain circled the slender neck with its thin gold line; the tapering hand, veined in blue, was holding a flower – a tea rose – whose petals were falling away and drifting to the ground like tears.

Alicia did not know her mother, who had died a year after giving birth to her; but she had often stood contemplating a miniature whose almost completely faded colours, with their yellow ivory tone, and as pale as the memory of the dead, made you think of the portrait of a shadow rather than that of a living woman, and she realised that this woman now coming into her room was Nancy Ward – her mother. The white dress, the Venetian chain, the flower in her hand, her black hair, her cheeks mottled with pink marble, it was all there – it really was the miniature, enlarged, solidified, moving with all the reality of a dream.

A mixture of love and terror made Alicia's heart beat faster. She wanted to hold out her arms to the shade, but her arms, as heavy as marble, were unable to rise from the couch on which they were resting. She tried to speak, but her tongue could stammer only a few confused syllables.

Nancy, having placed the tea rose on the pedestal table, knelt at the bedside and laid her head against Alicia's breast, listening to her lungs, counting her heartbeats; the shade's cold cheek gave the young woman, terrified by this silent examination, the sensation of a lump of ice.

The apparition rose again, cast a sorrowful glance at the young woman, and, counting the petals of the rose from which a few more petals had dropped, said, 'There is only one left.'

Then sleep had interposed its black gauze between the shade and the sleeper, and everything had been swallowed up in night.

Was her mother's soul coming to warn her and fetch her? What did that mysterious phrase fallen from the shade's lips mean: 'There is only one left'? Was this pale dishevelled rose the symbol of her life? This strange dream with its gracious terrors and its frightening charm, this enchanting spectre draped in muslin and counting the petals of flowers, preoccupied the young woman's imagination, a cloud of melancholy crossed her beautiful face and indefinable premonitions brushed her with their black wings.

Did this orange branch shaking its flowers over her also, perhaps, have some funereal meaning? And were the little maidenly stars not, after all, going to shine out beneath her bridal veil? Saddened and pensive, Alicia took from her lips the flower she had been nibbling; the flower was already yellow and withered...

The time for M. d'Aspremont's visit was approaching. Miss Ward made an effort to pull herself together, recomposed her face, gave the curls in her hair an extra twist, readjusted the crumpled folds of her gauze scarf, and picked up her book to make herself look at ease.

Paul came in, and Miss Ward received him playfully, not wanting him to be alarmed at finding her lying down, for he would not have failed to think himself the cause of her illness. The scene he had just had with Count Altavilla gave Paul a wild, angry expression, which provoked Vicè to make the protective gesture, but Alicia's affectionate smile had soon dispersed the cloud.

'You're not seriously ill, I hope,' he said to Miss Ward, sitting down at her side.

'Oh! it's nothing, I'm just a bit tired: the sirocco was blowing yesterday, and this wind from Africa really exhausts me; but you'll see how well I feel in our cottage in Lincolnshire! Now that I'm feeling stronger again, we'll each of us be able to take our turns at rowing out on the pond!'

As she said these words, she could not altogether suppress a little convulsive cough.

M. d'Aspremont turned pale and averted his eyes.

Silence reigned for a few minutes in the room.

'Paul, I've never given you anything,' resumed Alicia, taking from her already thin finger a simple gold ring; 'take this ring, and wear it in memory of me; you will perhaps be able to get it on, since you have a woman's hands. Goodbye! I'm feeling tired and would like to try and get some sleep; come and see me tomorrow.'

Paul withdrew, overcome by sorrow; Alicia's efforts to hide her suffering had been useless; he was deeply in love with Miss Ward, and he was killing her! Wasn't this ring she had just given him an engagement ring for the next life?

He wandered, half out of his wits, along the shore, dreaming of running away, of going off to bury himself in a Trappist monastery and there await death sitting on his coffin, without ever lifting up the hood of his habit. He felt that he was spiteful and cowardly not to sacrifice his love and to continue abusing Alicia's heroism like this: for nothing was hidden from her, she knew that he was nothing but a *jettatore*, as Count Altavilla had claimed, and, overwhelmed by angelic pity, she refused to reject him!

'Yes,' he said to himself, 'this Neapolitan, this handsome count whom she disdains, is really in love. His passion puts mine to shame: to save Alicia, he hasn't drawn back from attacking me, provoking me, a *jettatore*, in other words a being as frightful as a demon. Even as he spoke to me, he was playing with his amulets, and the eyes of that famous duellist, who has laid low three men, looked down when I gazed at him!'

Returning to the hotel Roma, Paul wrote several letters, drew up a testament in which he left to Miss Alicia Ward all that he possessed, except for a bequest for Paddy, and made the arrangements indispensable for a gentleman who is to fight a duel the next day.

He opened the rosewood boxes in which his weapons were enclosed, nestling in compartments lined with green serge, sorted through swords, pistols, and hunting knives, and finally found two perfectly identical Corsican stilettos which he had bought as presents for his friends.

They were two blades of pure steel, thick near the handle, sharp on both sides near the tip, damascened, curiously terrifying and mounted with great care. Paul also chose three scarves and wrapped everything up into a bundle.

Then he told Scazziga to be ready at daybreak for an excursion into the countryside.

'Oh!' he said, flinging himself fully clothed onto his bed, 'may God let this combat prove mortal to me! If I had the good fortune to be killed, Alicia would live!'

Pompeii, the dead city, doesn't wake up in the morning like living cities, and although it has half flung back the sheet of ashes which covered it for so many centuries, even when night fades, it remains asleep on its funereal bed.

The tourists of every nation who visit it during the day are at this hour still stretched out in their beds, stiff and sore from their exhausting excursions, and dawn, rising over the rubble of the mummified city, does not have a single human face to shine on. Only the lizards, their tails quivering, dart along the walls, flicker across the disjointed mosaics, without paying any attention to the *cave canem* inscribed on the thresholds of the deserted houses, and merrily greet the sun's first rays. These are the inhabitants who have succeeded the citizens of ancient times, and it seems that Pompeii has been exhumed for them alone.

It's a strange sight, in the azure and pink light of the morning, this corpse of a city overwhelmed in the midst of its pleasures, its labours, and its civilisation, and untouched by the slow dissolution of ordinary ruins; you can't help believing that the residents of these minutely preserved houses are about to emerge from their dwellings wearing their Greek or Roman clothes; the chariots, whose ruts you can still see on the flagstones, will start rolling along once more; the drinkers will walk into the *thermopoles*[29] where the mark of their cups still stains the marble of the counters. You walk as if dreaming through the past; you can read, in red letters, at street corners, the posters advertising that day's shows! – but the day is one that passed more than seventeen centuries ago. As the dawn slowly breaks, the dancing-girls painted on the walls seem to be shaking their castanets, and the tips of their white toes seem to be lifting like a pink foam the edge of their drapery, thinking no doubt that the *lampadaria* are being lit for yet another orgy in the *triclinium*;[30] the Venuses, the Satyrs, the heroic or grotesque figures brought to life by a sunbeam, try to take the place of the long-vanished inhabitants, and to make up a painted population for the dead city. The coloured shadows tremble along the walls, and for a few minutes your mind can lend itself to the illusion of an ancient phantasmagoria. But that particular day, to the great fright of the lizards, Pompeii's morning peace and tranquillity was disturbed by a strange visitor: a carriage halted at the entry to the Street of Tombs; Paul stepped out of it and headed on foot to the place of his assignation.

He was early, and although he must have been preoccupied by other things than archaeology, he could not stop himself, as he walked along, noting a thousand little details that he would perhaps not have noticed if he had found himself in any ordinary situation. The senses that are no longer under the surveillance of the soul, and can thus exercise themselves as they will, sometimes enjoy a remarkable lucidity. People sentenced to death, as they go to the scaffold, can distinguish a small flower in the cracks between the paving-stones, the number on a uniform button, a spelling mistake on a shop sign, or any other puerile circumstance which takes on a huge importance. M. d'Aspremont passed in front of the villa of Diomedes, the tomb of Mammia, the funerary hemicycles, the ancient city gate, the houses and shops that line the Consular Way, almost without having to look at them, and yet vivid, brightly coloured images of these monuments reached his brain with perfect distinctness; he could see everything: the fluted columns half-coated with red or yellow stucco, and the fresco paintings, and the inscriptions on the walls; an offer of rented accommodation in red chalk had even etched itself so deeply into his memory that his lips automatically repeated the Latin words without attaching any kind of meaning to them.

So was it the idea of his duel that was absorbing Paul to this extent? Not at all, he wasn't even thinking of it; his mind was elsewhere: in the parlour at Richmond. He was handing the commodore his letter of recommendation, and Miss Ward was looking at him secretively; she was wearing a white dress, and flowers of jasmine were strewn like stars in her hair. How young, beautiful and full of life she had been... then!

The ancient baths are at the end of the Consular Way, near the street of Fortune; M. d'Aspremont had no difficulty finding them. He walked into the vaulted room surrounded by a row of recesses formed by Atlas figures in terracotta, supporting an architrave decorated with children and foliage. The marble surfaces, the mosaics, the bronze tripods, have all disappeared. Nothing is left of the ancient splendour apart from the clay Atlas figures, and walls as bare as those of a tomb; a wan light, falling from a little round window which cuts a blue disc from the sky, falls tremulously onto the broken flags of the floor.

It was here that the women of Pompeii would come, after their bath, to dry their lovely wet bodies, adjust their hair, pick up their tunics and smile at themselves in the burnished copper of the mirrors. A scene of quite another kind was about to happen here, and blood was about to flow on the ground where once perfumes had streamed.

A few moments later Count Altavilla appeared: he was holding a pistol case in his hand, and carrying two swords under his arms, since he refused to believe that the conditions proposed by Paul were serious; he had seen them merely as a piece of Mephistophelean raillery, an infernal sarcasm.

'Why have you brought those pistols and swords, Count?' said Paul, seeing this armoury; 'hadn't we agreed on another mode of combat?'

'Doubtless; but I thought you might change your mind; no one has ever fought like that before.'

'Even if we were equal in skill, my position gives me too many advantages over you,' replied Paul, with a bitter smile; 'I don't want to abuse those advantages. Here are the stilettos I have brought; examine them; they are absolutely identical; here are scarves to act as blindfolds. Look, they are thick, and *my gaze* will be unable to pierce the fabric.'

Count Altavilla nodded in acquiescence.

'We have no seconds,' said Paul, 'and one of us must not emerge alive from this cellar. Let's each write a note attesting to the fact that the fight was in due and proper form; the victor will place it on the dead man's chest.'

'A wise precaution!' replied the Neapolitan with a smile, jotting down a few lines on a page of Paul's notebook; Paul in turn performed the same formality.

This done, the adversaries removed their jackets, blindfolded their eyes, armed themselves with their stilettos, and both seized one end of the handkerchief, the terrible hyphen between their two hatreds.

'Are you ready?' said M. d'Aspremont to Count Altavilla.

'Yes,' replied the Neapolitan in a perfectly calm voice.

Don Felipe Altavilla's bravery had been tried in combat, the only thing in the world he was afraid of was the jinx, and this blind combat, which would have made any other man shudder with dread, did not cause him the slightest disquiet; he was merely setting his life on the heads-or-tails of a tossed coin, and did not have the annoyance of seeing his enemy's wild eye darting its yellow stare at him.

The two combatants brandished their knives, and the handkerchief which linked them to each other in this thick darkness grew taut. Following an instinctive impulse, Paul and the Count had flung back their torsos, the single parry possible in this strange duel; their arms fell back without having struck anything more than thin air.

This obscure struggle, in which each of them could sense the imminence of death without being able to see it coming, was quite horrible in character. Fiercely intent and silent, the two opponents would recoil, spin round, jump up, sometimes collide, missing or overshooting their target; you could hear nothing but their heavy footfalls and the breath from their panting chests.

On one occasion Altavilla felt the tip of his stiletto make contact with something; he stopped, thinking he had killed his rival, and waited for the body to fall: he had merely struck the wall!

'Damn it! I thought I'd run you through,' he said, squaring up again.

'Don't talk,' said Paul, 'your voice will give your position away.'

And the combat resumed.

Suddenly the two opponents felt themselves separated. Paul's stiletto had cut through the scarf.

'A truce!' cried the Neapolitan; 'we're not attached any more, the handkerchief's been cut.'

'So what? let's carry on!' said Paul.

A melancholy silence fell. As worthy opponents, neither M. d'Aspremont nor the Count wished to take advantage of the indications given by their exchange of words. They took a few steps to disorientate themselves, and started once more to pursue each other in the dark.

M. d'Aspremont's foot dislodged a small stone; its faint clatter revealed to the Neapolitan, waving his knife at random, which direction he should walk in. Tensing his legs to give himself more momentum, Altavilla sprang forward like a tiger and ran straight onto the stiletto of M. d'Aspremont.

Paul touched the tip of his weapon and realised it was wet… tottering steps echoed heavily on the flags; an oppressed sigh was heard and a body fell in a heap to the ground.

Overwhelmed with horror, Paul tore away the blindfold from his eyes, and saw Count Altavilla, pale, motionless, sprawled on his back, his shirt stained where his heart was by a broad pool of red.

The handsome Neapolitan was dead!

M. d'Aspremont placed on Altavilla's chest the note attesting to the fairness of the duel, and left the ancient baths, his face paler in the sunlight than is the criminal depicted by Prud'hon pursued by avenging Erinnyes by the light of the moon.[31]

CHAPTER FOURTEEN

At around two o'clock in the afternoon, a band of English tourists, guided by a *cicerone*, was visiting the ruins of Pompeii; the insular tribe, composed of the father, the mother, three grown-up daughters, two small sons and a cousin, had already looked over, with their cold, dull, blue-green eyes, in which could be read that profound boredom characteristic of the British race, the amphitheatre, the theatre of tragedies and song, so curiously juxtaposed; the military quarters, graffitied by caricatures scrawled by guards at a loose end; the Forum, which they found undergoing repairs; the basilica, the temples of Venus and Jupiter, the Pantheon, and the shops which line these buildings. They were all silently following the long-winded explanations of the *cicerone* in their *Murray's Guide* and hardly even glancing at the columns, the fragments of statues, the mosaics, the frescoes and the inscriptions.

Finally they reached the ancient baths, discovered in 1824, as the guide pointed out to them. 'Here were the steam rooms, there the furnace to heat the water, further on the warm-water baths'; these details given in Neapolitan patois mixed with a few English endings seemed of little interest to the visitors, who were already doing an about-turn to make their way back, when Miss Ethelwina, the oldest of the young ladies, a young woman with dirty yellow hair, and skin freckled like a trout, took two steps backwards, looking half shocked and half frightened, and exclaimed: 'A man!'

'It's probably a workman employed on the excavations who thought this was a good spot for a siesta; under this vault there's plenty of freshness and shade: don't be afraid, miss,' said the guide, prodding the body lying on the ground with his foot. 'Hey! wake up, lazybones, and let their lordships come by.'

The apparent sleeper didn't move.

'It's not a man having a siesta, it's a dead man,' said one of the boys who, thanks to his small stature, was better able in the shadows to make out the figure of the corpse.

The *cicerone* bent over the body and suddenly straightened up, his features expressing shock.

'A murdered man!' he exclaimed.

'Oh, it is so disagreeable to find oneself in the presence of such things; come away, Ethelwina, Kitty, Bess,' said Mrs Bracebridge. 'It is not right for well-brought-up young people to look at such an improper spectacle. There doesn't seem to be any police in this country! The coroner should have had the body taken in.'

'A piece of paper!' said the cousin laconically, who was stiff, long and awkward of character like the laird of Dumbidike in *The Heart of Midlothian*.[32]

'Indeed,' said the guide, picking up the note placed on Altavilla's chest, a piece of paper with a few lines of writing on it.

'Read it,' chorused those members of the island race, their curiosity greatly excited.

No one is to be sought or harassed for my death. If this note is found on my wound, I will have succumbed in a duel fought in due and proper form.

(Signed)
– Felipe, Count of Altavilla

'He was a respectable man; what a shame!' sighed Mrs Bracebridge, impressed by the dead man's status as a count.

'And a handsome young thing,' murmured Ethelwina, the young lady with the freckles, in a low voice.

'You won't complain again that our travels lack the occasional surprise,' said Bess to Kitty. 'We haven't, it's true, been stopped by brigands on the road between Terracina and Fondi; but a young man pierced by a stiletto in the ruins of Pompeii, now that *is* an adventure. No doubt there's some love rivalry behind it all; at least we'll have something Italianate, picturesque and romantic, to tell our friends. I will do a drawing of the scene in my album, and you can embellish the sketch with some mysterious stanzas in the style of Byron.'

'It makes no odds,' said the guide, 'the blow was dealt properly, from bottom to top, in accordance with all the rules; there's no cause for complaint.'

Such was the funeral oration spoken over Count Altavilla.

A few labourers, alerted by the *cicerone*, went to fetch the officers of the law, and poor Altavilla's body was taken back to his estate, near Salerno.

As for M. d'Aspremont, he had returned to his carriage, his eyes wide open like those of a sleepwalker, seeing nothing. He looked like a walking statue. Although he had felt at the sight of the corpse that religious horror which death inspires in us, he did not feel guilty, and remorse played no part at all in his despair. Provoked in such a way that he could not refuse, he had accepted the duel simply hoping that it would enable him to leave a life that was henceforth hateful to him. Endowed with a harmful gaze, he had chosen blind combat so that fate alone would be responsible. His hand, indeed, had not even struck the blow; his enemy had impaled himself! He pitied Count Altavilla as if he had had nothing to do with his death. 'It's my stiletto that killed him,' he said to himself, 'but if I had looked at him during a ball, a chandelier would have come loose from the ceiling and split his skull open. I am as innocent as the lightning, the avalanche, or the manchineel tree, as are all destructive and unconscious forces. My will has never wished harm to anyone, my heart is nothing but love and benevolence, and yet I know that I am pernicious. The lightning doesn't know that it kills; but do not I, a man, an intelligent creature, have a strict duty to fulfil towards myself? I must arraign myself before my own tribunal and cross-question myself. Can I remain on this earth where I cause nothing but misfortune? Would God damn me if I killed myself out of love for my kind? A terrible, profound question which I dare not try to answer; it seems to me that, in the position I am in, self-inflicted death is excusable. But what if I were wrong? For the whole of eternity, I would be deprived of the sight of Alicia, just when I would be able to look at her without harming her, for the eyes of the soul have no *fascino*. It's a risk I don't want to take.'

A sudden idea flashed through the brain of the unhappy *jettatore* and interrupted his inner monologue. His features relaxed; the unshakeable serenity that follows great resolutions smoothed his pale brow: he had come to a supreme decision.

'Stand condemned, my eyes, since you are murderous; but, before closing for ever, saturate yourselves in light, contemplate the sun, the blue sky, the immense sea, the blue-hazed mountain ranges, the trees with their green leaves, the horizons stretching out for ever, the colonnades of palaces, the fisherman's shack, the islands far out in the gulf, the white sail scudding over the abyss, Vesuvius, with its plume of smoke; gaze at all those enchanting aspects that you will never see again, and imprint them on your memory; study each shape and each colour, indulge yourselves in one final festivity. For today, whether you are harmful or not, your eyes may rest on everything; drink your fill of the intoxicating splendour of the spectacle of Creation! Go on, have a good look, gaze all around you. The curtain will soon be falling between you and the scenery of the world!'

The carriage, at this moment, was driving along the shore; the radiant bay was sparkling, the sky seemed cut from a single sapphire; all things were clothed in a splendour of beauty.

Paul asked Scazziga to stop; he stepped down, sat on a rock and gazed for a long, long, long time, as if he had been trying to hoard up the infinite in his gaze. His eyes sank into the vastness of space and light, rolled inwards as if in ecstasy, drenched themselves in the brilliant glow, drank in the sun! The night that was to follow would not, for him, be followed by any dawn.

Tearing himself away from this silent contemplation, M. d'Aspremont climbed back into his carriage and went to see Miss Alicia Ward.

She was lying, as she had been the previous day, on her narrow sofa, in the lower room we have already described. Paul stood opposite her, and this time did not keep his eyes fixed on the ground, as he had been doing ever since he had become aware of his jinx.

Alicia's perfect beauty was spiritualised by suffering: the woman had almost disappeared to give way to the angel. Her flesh was transparent, ethereal, luminous; you could see her soul through it, like a light flickering inside an alabaster lamp. Her eyes had in them the infinite expanse of the sky and the glitter of stars; life had barely set its red signature to her body in the incarnadine of her lips.

A divine smile lit up her mouth, like a ray of sunlight shining on a rose, when she saw her fiancé's eyes enveloping her in a long caress. She thought that Paul had finally rid himself of his gloomy jinx-haunted notions and was returning to her happy and self-confident as in the first days, and she extended to M. d'Aspremont, who kept it in his, her pale and tapering little hand.

'So I don't frighten you any more?' she said, with gentle mockery to Paul who was still gazing fixedly at her.

'Oh, let me look at you!' replied M. d'Aspremont, in a strange tone of voice, falling to his knees beside the sofa; 'let me drink my fill of that ineffable and intoxicating beauty!' and he continued to contemplate avidly Alicia's lustrous black hair, her lovely forehead as pure as Greek marble, her blue-black eyes like the deep azure of a fine night sky, her finely sculpted nose, her mouth whose languid smile half displayed its pearly teeth, her swanlike sinuous and supple neck – and he seemed to note each feature, each detail, each perfection like a painter intent on painting a portrait from memory; he was gorging himself on her adored figure, building up a stock of memories, fixing her profile and catching every outline.

Beneath this ardent gaze, Alicia, fascinated and charmed, felt a sensation of voluptuous pain, delightful and deadly; her life was intensifying and fading away; she was blushing and growing pale, turning cold and then burning hot. A minute later, her soul would have left her.

She placed her hand over Paul's eyes, but the young man's gaze burnt through Alicia's frail, transparent hands like a flame.

'Now my eyes can be quenched, I will always see her in my heart,' said Paul, rising to his feet.

That evening, after watching the sunset – the last he was ever to see – M. d'Aspremont, on returning to the hotel Roma, had a stove and some coal brought up to him.

'Does he want to suffocate himself?' Virgilio Falsacappa said to himself, handing over to Paddy the equipment the latter had come to fetch for his master; 'it would be the best thing he could do, that cursed *jettatore*!'

Alicia's fiancé opened the window, quite contrary to Falsacappa's conjecture, lit the coals, thrust a dagger's blade into them and waited for the iron to get red-hot.

The slender blade, laid between the incandescent coals, had soon reached white heat; Paul, as if to bid himself farewell, propped himself up on his elbows on the mantelpiece looking into a great mirror on which fell the gleam of a candlestick with several burning candles; he gazed at that spectral figure in front of him, that husk of his thoughts which he would never see again, with melancholy curiosity. 'Farewell, pale phantom that I have been dragging round through life for so many years, a botched and sinister shape in which beauty and horror are mixed, clay that bears on its brow a fateful seal, the convulsed mask of a sweet and tender soul! You are going to disappear for ever from my sight: while still living, I am going to thrust you into eternal darkness, and soon I will have forgotten you like the dream of a stormy night. You can plead as you will, wretched body, with my inflexible will: 'Hubert, Hubert, my poor eyes!',[33] you won't soften its resolve. Come then, to work, victim and executioner!' And he left the mantelpiece and went to sit on the edge of his bed.

He breathed fresh heat into the coals of the stove placed on a nearby pedestal table, and grasped by the handle the blade from which white sparks were flashing and sputtering.

At this supreme moment, however great his resolve, M. d'Aspremont felt almost on the point of fainting: a cold sweat bathed his temples; but he rapidly overcame this purely physical wavering and brought the burning iron up to his eyes.

A sharp, stabbing, intolerable pain almost drew a cry from him; it seemed to him that two jets of molten lead were piercing through his eyes right to the back of his skull; he dropped the dagger, which tumbled to the ground and left a brown stain on the parquet floor.

A thick, dense shadow, next to which the darkest night was as bright as broad daylight, wrapped its black hood round his head; he turned his head towards the mantelpiece on which the candles must still be burning; he saw only thick, impenetrable darkness, not even dispelled by those tremulous flickers that full-sighted people can still perceive through closed eyes when they are facing a light. The sacrifice was accomplished!

'Now,' said Paul, 'noble and charming creature, I can become your husband without being an assassin. You will no longer waste heroically away beneath my fateful gaze: you will recover your robust health; alas! I won't be able to see you any longer, but your heavenly image will gleam with immortal radiance in my memory; I will see you with the eyes of the soul, I will hear your voice, more melodious than the sweetest music, I will sense the air set in motion by your movements, I will catch the silken rustle of your dress, the imperceptible creak of your laced boot, I will breathe in the delicate perfume that emanates from you and acts as a kind of atmosphere enveloping you. Sometimes you will leave your hand between mine to convince me you are really there, you will condescend to guide your poor blind man when his foot hesitates on his dark path; you will read the poets to him, you will tell the stories depicted by paintings and statues. Through your word, you will restore the vanished world to him; you will be his sole thought, his sole dream; deprived of the distraction of mere objects and the blinding gleam of light, his soul will fly towards you on tireless wings!

'I regret nothing, since you are saved: and what, after all, have I lost? The monotonous spectacle of the seasons and the days, the view of the more or less picturesque décors against which the hundred various acts of the sad human comedy are performed. The earth, the sky, the lakes and rivers, the mountains, the trees, the flowers: vain apparitions, tedious repetitions, never-changing shapes! When we have love, we possess the true sun, the bright glow that never fades!'

So spoke, in his inner monologue, the unfortunate Paul d'Aspremont, fired with feverish lyrical exaltation sometimes suffused by the delirium of suffering.

Little by little his pain subsided; he fell into that dark sleep that is the brother of death and, like death, consoling.

The light of day, falling into the room, did not awaken him. Midday and midnight would, from now on, have the same colour for him; but the bells ringing the Angelus in joyous peals tolled indistinctly through his slumber, and, gradually becoming clearer, drew him out of his drowsiness.

He lifted his eyelids, and, before his still sleepy soul could yet remember, he felt a terrible sensation. His eyes had opened onto emptiness, blackness, nothingness, as if he had been buried alive and were waking from his lethargy in a coffin; but he soon recovered. Wouldn't it always be like this? Wouldn't he have to pass, each morning, from the darkness of sleep to the darkness of the waking state?

He groped his way to the cord of his bell.

Paddy rushed in.

As he was expressing his astonishment at seeing his master getting up with the uncertain movements of a blind man, Paul spoke.

'I have been so unwise as to sleep with the window open,' Paul told him, to cut short any explanation, 'and I think I've caught a touch of amaurosis, but it won't last; lead me to my armchair and put a glass of fresh water next to it.'

Paddy, who had a perfectly English discretion, made no comment, carried out his master's orders, and withdrew.

Left alone, Paul dipped his handkerchief in the cold water, and held it to his eyes to deaden the hot pain caused by the burn.

Let us leave M. d'Aspremont in his painful immobility and give some attention to the other characters in our story.

The news of the strange death of Count Altavilla had quickly spread through Naples and was the theme of a thousand conjectures each one more far-fetched than the last. The Count's skill in fencing was known to all; Altavilla was considered one of the best marksmen of that Neapolitan school so formidable in the field; he had killed three men and seriously wounded five or six. His fame in this area was so well-established that he no longer fought. The most experienced duellists greeted him politely and, if he had given them a sideways glance, avoided stepping on his toes. If one of these braggarts had killed Altavilla, he wouldn't have hesitated to glory in such a victory. That left the suspicion of a murder, which was however eradicated by the note found on the dead man's chest. At first the authenticity of the hand-writing was questioned; but the Count's hand was recognised by people who had received more than a hundred letters from him. The circumstance of the blindfolded eyes, as the corpse was still wearing a scarf knotted around his head, still seemed impossible to explain. They found, apart from the stiletto stuck in the Count's chest, a second stiletto which had doubtless fallen from his failing hand: but if the combat had been fought with knives, why were those swords and pistols there, which were recognised as having belonged to the Count, whose own coachman declared that he had brought his master to Pompeii with orders to go home alone if at the end of an hour he did not reappear?

It was an inextricable labyrinth.

The rumour of this death soon reached the ears of Vicè, who informed Sir Joshua Ward of it. The commodore, who immediately recalled the mysterious conversation Altavilla had had with him about Alicia, confusedly imagined some dark murder plot, some horrible and desperate struggle in which M. d'Aspremont must be wittingly or unwittingly mixed up. As for Vicè, she didn't hesitate to attribute the death of the handsome Count to the villainous *jettatore*, and in this her hatred gave her the power of second sight. And yet M. d'Aspremont had come to visit Miss Ward at the accustomed hour, and nothing in his countenance had betrayed the emotion of a terrible drama, he had even appeared more calm than usual.

This death was kept hidden from Miss Ward, whose state of health was giving cause for concern, without the English doctor called by Sir Joshua being able to discover any clear illness: it was like a draining away of life, a palpitation of the soul beating its wings to take its flight, a bird suffocating in an air-pump, rather than a real malady susceptible to treatment by ordinary means. She looked like an angel detained on earth and longing to return to heaven; the beauty of Alicia was so sweet, so delicate, so diaphanous, so immaterial, that she could no longer breathe in this coarse human atmosphere; you could imagine her hovering in the golden light of Paradise, and the little lace pillow supporting her head gleamed like a halo. As she lay on her bed, she resembled that charming little Virgin by Scorel[34], the most delicate jewel of Gothic art.

M. d'Aspremont did not come that day: to hide his sacrifice, he did not want to appear with his eyelids reddened, keeping open the possibility of attributing his sudden blindness to some quite different cause.

The following day, no longer feeling any pain, he climbed into his carriage, guided by his groom Paddy.

The carriage halted as usual at the gate. The self-blinded man pushed it open and, feeling his way with his feet, made his way along the well-known path. Vicè had not come running up in her usual way at the ringing of the bell set jangling by the springs of the gate; none of those thousand little sounds that are like the breathing of a living house reached Paul's attentive ear; a deep, gloomy, frightening silence reigned throughout the dwelling, which you might have thought was abandoned. This silence, which would have been sinister even for a man who could see clearly, became even more mournful in the darkness enveloping the newly blind man.

The branches that he could no longer distinguish seemed to be trying to hold him back like supplicant arms and stop him from going any further. The laurels barred his way; the rose branches caught on his clothes, the creepers wrapped themselves round his legs, the garden said to him in its mute language, 'Unhappy man! What are you coming here for? Don't force your way through the obstacles that are holding you back, go away!' But Paul didn't listen and, tortured by terrible premonitions, staggered and tripped through the foliage, thrusting back the masses of greenery, crashing through the branches and continuing to push his way towards the house.

Torn and bruised by the angry branches, he finally reached the end of the path. A gust of fresh air blew into his face, and he continued on his way holding his hands out ahead of him.

He came up against the wall and groped his way to the door.

He went in; no friendly voice bid him welcome. Hearing no sound to guide him, he remained for a few minutes hesitating on the threshold. The smell of ether, the exhalation of aromatic herbs and spices, the odour of melting wax, all the vague perfumes of rooms in which someone has just died invaded the sense of smell of the blind man as he gasped with dread; a terrible idea came to his mind, and he entered the room.

After a few steps, he bumped into something which fell with a great clatter; he stooped down and recognised by touch that it was a metal candlestick with a long candle like those used in church.

In a panic, he continued on his way through the darkness. He thought he heard a low voice murmuring prayers; he took another step, and his hands made contact with the edge of a bed; he leant forward, and his trembling fingers grazed first a motionless body stretched out under a fine tunic, then a crown of roses and a face pure and cold as marble.

It was Alicia lying on her funeral couch.

'Dead!' cried Paul with a strangled gasp, 'dead! and it is I who killed her!'

The commodore, frozen with horror, had seen this phantom with its empty eyes enter on tottering legs, wander round uncertainly and bump into his niece's deathbed: he had understood everything. The grandeur of this useless sacrifice made two tears spring from the old man's reddened eyes, who had thought he had no more tears to shed.

Paul dropped to his knees at the bedside and covered with kisses Alicia's icy hand; sobs were shaking his body in convulsive spasms. His grief even softened the heart of the fierce Vicè, who was standing silent and sombre against the wall, keeping vigil over her mistress' last sleep.

When this mute farewell was at an end, M. d'Aspremont stood up and moved towards the door, stiff, jerky, like an automaton moved by springs; his open staring eyes, with their lifeless appearance, had a supernatural expression; though blind, they seemed to see. He crossed the garden with a heavy tread like that of marble apparitions, headed out into the countryside and walked straight ahead, knocking the stones out of his way, sometimes staggering, his ears pricked as if to catch a sound in the distance, but continuing to move forward.

The great voice of the sea sounded more and distinct; the waves, whipped up by a stormy wind, were crashing against the shore with immense sobs that expressed unknown sorrows, and, under the folds of foam, baring their swollen and despairing breasts; millions of bitter tears dripped from the rocks, and the disquieted seagulls were wailing plaintively.

Paul soon reached the edge of a rock which overlooked the sea. The din of the waves, the salty drizzle which the gusts of wind were tearing from the waves and throwing into his face should have warned him of the danger; he paid it no attention; his pale lips were compressed in a strange smile, and he continued his sinister progress, despite sensing the void beneath his lifted foot.

He fell; a monstrous wave seized him, twisted him for a few seconds in its vortex, and swallowed him up.

Then the tempest broke out in fury: the breakers assailed the beach in serried ranks, like warriors launching an attack, and sending foaming spray hurtling fifty feet into the air; the black clouds were split apart like the walls of hell, showing through their fissures the fiery furnace of the lightning; sulphurous, blinding flashes lit up the entire scene; the summit of Vesuvius turned red, and a plume of dark vapour, forced upwards by the contrary wind, billowed from the volcano's brow. The moored boats ground into one another with mournful groans, and the ropes, overstrained, moaned plaintively. Soon the rain fell in dense streams, cross-hatched and hissing like arrows – it was as if chaos wanted to regain control of nature and bring its elements into confusion once more.

M. Paul d'Aspremont's body was never found, despite all the searches carried out at the commodore's request.

A coffin of ebony, with clasps and handles of silver, lined with padded satin, of just the same sort, in fact, as the one recommended in detail by Miss Clarissa Harlowe, with such touching grace, to 'Mr Carpenter', was put on board a yacht by the good offices of the commodore, and placed in the family vault near the Lincolnshire cottage. It contained the earthly remains of Alicia Ward, beautiful even in death.

As for the commodore, a remarkable change has come about in his person. His glorious stoutness has disappeared. He no longer puts rum in his tea, he picks at his food, says barely two words all day long, and the contrast between his white side-whiskers and his crimson face no longer exists – the commodore has become pale!

1. 'Porters' in Italian.

2. An episode from *Télémaque* (c. 1695) by Fénelon, loosely based on Homer's *Odyssey*.

3. The Studii is the archaeological museum in Naples.

4. Celebrated British boxers.

5. Don Quixote's broken-down nag.

6. 'Water-sellers' in Italian.

7. 'Carriages' in Neapolitan dialect. Alexandre Dumas's 'Le Corricolo' includes a chapter on the jinx and may have influenced Gautier's story.

8. John Frederick Lewis (1805–76) was a British watercolourist.

9. Daniel Maclise (1806–70) was an Irish painter and portraitist.

10. Donizetti's *Lucia di Lammermoor* was first performed in the San Carlo theatre in Naples (1835); '*Te voglio ben' assai*' is 'I love you deeply' in Neapolitan dialect.

11. '*Carlini*', 'ducats' and 'grani' were the currency of nineteenth-century Naples.

12. *Anna Bolena* was Donizetti's first opera (1830).

13. 'Stranger' in Neapolitan dialect.

14. '*Trovatella*' is 'foundling' in Italian; Luigi Gordigiani (1814–60) was a Florentine composer.

15. The approximate Italian equivalent of Punch.

16. Roman emperor Vitellius was famous for his appetite.

17. An Italian cow's-milk cheese.

18. The patron saint of Naples.

19. '*Tutto da ridere*' means 'hilarious' in Italian; '*lazzi*' are jests or witticisms.

20. Someone with the power of '*jettatura*', the jinx or evil eye.

21. Thomas Moore (1779–1852) was an Irish poet, famous for his satires and ballads.

22. *The Body Language of the Ancients as it is Studied in Neapolitan Gesticulations* (1832).

23. A character from Byron's poem *Don Juan* (1819–24) who lived in a harem.

24. A bizarre creature in Charles Nodier's fantastic story (1821) of that name.

25. Nicola Valetta (1738–1814) was an Italian professor of civil and Roman law. His *Cicalata sul fascino volgarmente detto jettatura* (*A Discussion of the Spell Commonly Called 'Jettatura'*) was published in Naples in 1787.

26. 'Oyster-seller' in Italian.

27. 'Public baths' in Latin.

28. Andrea Meldolla, alias Schiavone (1515–63), was an Italian painter.

29. 'Taverns' in Greek.

30. '*Lampadaria*' and '*triclinium*' are 'ceiling lamps' and 'dining room' in Latin.

31. Pierre Paul Prud'hon (1758–1832)'s painting *Justice and Divine Vengeance Pursuing Crime* is in the Louvre.

32. Sir Walter Scott's novel was published in 1818.

33. Gautier is here referring to Shakespeare's *King John* (IV. i).

34. Jan van Scorel (1495–1562) was a Dutch painter.

Théophile Gautier was born in the Pyrenees in 1811 but was brought up in Paris. As a teenager Gautier trained to be a painter until he met Victor Hugo, who inspired him to become a poet. He published his first volume of poetry when he was only nineteen, and from then on, as he put it proudly, he 'lived by his pen alone'.

Gautier is perhaps best-known for having coined, in 1835, the theory of 'art for art's sake' (in the preface to his first novel, *Mademoiselle de Maupin*). But despite his artistic ethics, he never made enough money to exist solely as a poet. Gautier had several children, ran a large establishment (his '*ménagerie intime*') and was forced, for financial reasons, to work as a journalist. Introduced by his friend Balzac to the editor of the *Chronique de Paris* at a young age, Gautier quickly made his name as critic, contributing to the *Figaro* and *La Presse*, and writing a celebrated theatre column with his friend Gérard de Nerval for fourteen years. In 1840 Gautier travelled around post-war Spain, an experience which deeply moved him, and which he described in his first travel-book, *Tra-los-Montès*. Gautier's most popular works were his ballets; his first and most famous was *Giselle*, which is still performed today. Poetry, however, was his abiding literary passion and his own poetic reputation rests on his last volume of poetry, *Emaux et camées* [*Enamels and Cameos*] (1852).

Gautier's original mind and large literary output made him a key figure in the nineteenth-century French Romanticist movement. He received the *Légion d'honneur*, but to his regret, was never accepted as a member of the *Académie française*, despite being nominated by Sainte-Beuve and Mérimée. He died in 1872.

Andrew Brown studied at the University of Cambridge, where he taught French for many years. He now works as a freelance teacher and translator. He is the author of *Roland Barthes: the Figures of Writing* (OUP, 1993), and various translations of works relating to French history and philosophy.

HESPERUS PRESS – 100 PAGES

Hesperus Press, as suggested by the Latin motto, is committed to bringing near what is far – far both in space and time. Works written by the greatest authors, and unjustly neglected or simply little known in the English-speaking world, are made accessible through new translations and a completely fresh editorial approach. Through these short classic works, each little more than 100 pages in length, the reader will be introduced to the greatest writers from all times and all cultures.

For more information on Hesperus Press, please visit our website:
www.hesperuspress.com

To place an order, please contact:
Grantham Book Services, Isaac Newton Way
Alma Park Industrial Estate
Grantham, Lincolnshire NG31 9SD
Tel: +44 (0) 1476 541080 Fax: +44 (0) 1476 541061
Email: orders@gbs.tbs-ltd.co.uk

SELECTED TITLES FROM HESPERUS PRESS

Gustave Flaubert *Memoirs of a Madman*
Alexander Pope *Scriblerus*
Ugo Foscolo *Last Letters of Jacopo Ortis*
Anton Chekhov *The Story of a Nobody*
Joseph von Eichendorff *Life of a Good-for-nothing*
Mark Twain *The Diary of Adam and Eve*
Giovanni Boccaccio *Life of Dante*
Victor Hugo *The Last Day of a Condemned Man*
Joseph Conrad *Heart of Darkness*
Edgar Allan Poe *Eureka*
Emile Zola *For a Night of Love*
Daniel Defoe *The King of Pirates*
Giacomo Leopardi *Thoughts*

Nikolai Gogol *The Squabble*
Franz Kafka *Metamorphosis*
Herman Melville *The Enchanted Isles*
Leonardo da Vinci *Prophecies*
Charles Baudelaire *On Wine and Hashish*
William Makepeace Thackeray *Rebecca and Rowena*
Wilkie Collins *Who Killed Zebedee?*
Charles Dickens *The Haunted House*
Luigi Pirandello *Loveless Love*
Fyodor Dostoevsky *Poor People*
E.T.A. Hoffmann *Mademoiselle de Scudéri*
Henry James *In the Cage*
Francis Petrarch *My Secret Book*
André Gide *Theseus*
D.H. Lawrence *The Fox*
Percy Bysshe Shelley *Zastrozzi*